Catwalk:
A Feline Odyssey

Copyright © by Bill MacDonald
and Borealis Press Ltd., 2006

All rights reserved. No part of this book may be used or reproduced in any manner whatsoever without prior written permission from the Publisher, except in the case of brief quotations embodied in critical articles and reviews.

Canadä

The Publishers acknowledge the financial assistance of the Government of Canada through the Book Publishing Industry Development Program (BPIDP) for our publishing activities.

Library and Archives Canada Cataloguing in Publication

MacDonald, Bill, 1932-
  Catwalk : a feline odyssey / Bill MacDonald.

ISBN 0-88887-326-3

  I. Title.

PS8575.D668C38 2006   C813'.54   C2006-904767-7

Cover design by Bull's Eye Design, Ottawa
Printed and bound in Canada on acid free paper.

Catwalk:
A Feline Odyssey

Bill MacDonald

Borealis Press
Ottawa, Canada
2006

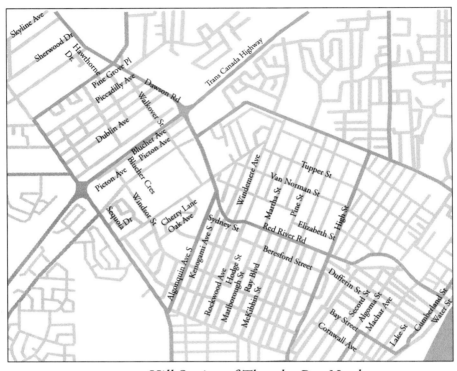

Hill Section of Thunder Bay North

Previous Borealis books by this author:

*The Great Millennium Mount Everest Cat Expedition
& Other Cat Stories*

Home Before Dark

Patagonian Odyssey

Goodbye Piccadilly

Hyenas in the Streets

Daughters of the Sun

Clowns in the Closet

Vive Zigoto!

Christmas Eve at Silver Islet

Stinging Nettles

The Holly Tree

Soothsayer

Barnabas Snug Harbour

CONTENTS

ONE	First Steps: Skyline Avenue to Hawthorne Drive	3
TWO	An Evening with Queenie and Priapus	11
THREE	Hattie and the Sandsuckers	23
FOUR	Just Can't Wait to Get on the Road Again	33
FIVE	Christmas with Theo and His Yellow Pine Coffin	43
SIX	Green-Eyed Angela and the Trafalgar of Neebing Marsh	55
SEVEN	A Night with Alexi in the Basement of St Elmo's Church, Another in Hildegarde's Cubbyhole in the Coach House of St Joseph's Manor	67
EIGHT	Hector, Martha and Bertha, Giuseppe's Gold Mercedes	87
NINE	Stopover at Barnabas Safe Haven with Ursula	101
TEN	Juan Escobar, the Bughouse Bar & Grill, Britney, Grandma Nelly's Farewell	121
ELEVEN	Home at Last! Venetia Agrippa and Jailbird Neville	135
TWELVE	Theo the Canoe- and Coffin-Maker Revisited	147

ONE
First Steps: Skyline Avenue to Hawthorne Drive

c a t n. **1.** a small, soft-furred, flesh-eating domesticated mammal, *Felis catus*, having a short snout and retractile claws, and kept as a pet or for catching mice. **2.** a wild member of the family *Felidae*, which includes the lion, tiger, lynx, leopard, puma, cheetah and ocelot. **3.** a spiteful or malicious woman. **4.** a jazz enthusiast.

—*Oxford English Reference Dictionary*

To begin with, I'd like it known that I fall into the first category. At least I think I do. I'm not very big, my fur is fairly soft, and I like meat. Whether I'm domesticated or not is a matter of opinion. I don't believe I possess a snout, however. What I have is a nose. If retractile means you can hide your claws, then that's me. As for being a pet, I'll leave that for you to judge. With regard to catching mice, I'm pretty good, considering my lack of practice. And while I may bear a slight resemblance to a male lion, I don't have a mane and I can't roar. I've tried, and it's hopeless. I can caterwaul with the best of them, but I can't roar. You'd never mistake me for a lynx, either. My ears are untufted and I have small feet. So although I'm stealthy, I don't think I qualify as a wild member of Felidae. Neither am I a jazz enthusiast nor a spiteful woman. What I am, by definition, is Felis catus—the common, or not so common, house cat. For which I make no apologies. My name, by the way, is Rufus. That's what my sweet Guinevere has called me, ever since I can remember. It was also she who first read me the above dictionary definition of cats, one day when I was confined to bed with the punies.

Let's be clear about one thing: I've no intention of trying to justify walking all the way from Skyline Avenue in Jumbo Gardens down to Lake Street on the waterfront. Nor, by the same token, will I brag about it. If it strikes you as a dumb endeavour, fine. The thing is, I did it. Not as quickly as I could have, perhaps, but still, I did it. You won't see my name in the *Guinness Book of World Records*. Lots of cats have walked further, faster. Guinevere once read me a story about an Egyptian shorthair named Minya, who holds the record. Minya lived around 2780 BC and was owned by a pyramid builder's wife, a renowned potter from Thebes named Zagazig, whose ceramic vessels were in demand during the Nubian dynasty. I assume they were put inside tombs with mummies. One winter Minya walked from Cairo to Aswan, which is a little over 600 kilometres. On the way back, she got a lift as far as Luxor with a camel caravan, because cars hadn't been invented yet.

My own little trek took me the better part of six months.

Too slow, you say? Well, maybe. Compared to Minya's feat, I suppose it was. But still, how many *Felis cati* do you know who have made such a trek? Without a map, without a compass. Without radar or GPS. And don't forget, it took Odysseus ten years to get back to Ithaca.

When I set off on Thanksgiving weekend, it seemed like a good idea. A worthwhile idea. A walk in the park. How difficult could it be? Had I known it was forty-four blocks (five kilometres, or three and a half miles), across a divided highway, two arterial thoroughfares and a dozen busy intersections, I might have thought twice. Had I known I'd need to take a total of 75,000 steps, at an average of 12,500 steps per month, I might have reconsidered. That's a lot of walking for a cat. It doesn't leave much time for eating, sleeping and socializing. Mind you, 12,500 steps per month is an average. Some months I did more, some months less. Weather was also a factor. So were social obligations. A lot depended on the availability of accommodations and how well I was received. Lacking credit cards, I couldn't just stop and grab a bite at McDonald's or the Brew Pub. If it was raining and my feet hurt, I couldn't just check into the Ramada Inn and say, "I'd like a room, please."

En route, I was delayed for a variety of reasons. Some days I got sidetracked. I'm curious by nature, and there were things to do, places to see. For example, on my very first day, at the corner of Pine Grove Place and Dawson Road, I discovered a patch of wild mint. Next to Colombian catnip, that's my favourite herb, and so I took time out for a visit. Which is what any sane cat would do. There were six or seven of us, cavorting among the fallen leaves, getting acquainted. It was a golden autumn afternoon and time seemed to stand still. There was no turmoil, no aggression. Things were calm. I remember a svelte orange part-Persian named Phyllis asking me if I lived thereabouts. I said, "No, I'm just passing through. I'm on my way home to the Bayview Apartments on Lake Street. After a family crisis, I was handed over, for reasons I won't bore you with, to people who did little more than feed me. So I have this urge . . ."

But Phyllis wasn't all that interested. She was too busy rolling in the leaves, messing up her hairdo. Finally, admiring my flea collar, she said, "This might not be the best time of year for a pilgrimage, dude. What with winter coming on. Seems to me it might better be done in summer. It's like white-water rafting. I see hidden dangers in your path. What if you don't make it before the snow flies? That's a long journey over hostile terrain. You'll have to pass gas stations, a fire house, three or four strip malls. Not to mention Tim Horton's drive-through and a car wash. And what will you do about food and shelter? Were you terribly unhappy on Skyline Avenue?"

I had to stop and think about this. I said, "Well, no, I wasn't all that unhappy. I had a roof over my head and a litter box in the basement. But the old couple I lived with, Guinevere's aunt and uncle, didn't dote on cats the way she did. They chastised me for digging holes in the garden. I mean, what's a garden for? Plus, they were finicky about where I regurgitated fur balls and which chairs I sharpened my claws on. They disapproved of me sitting in the sink or on the kitchen table. They left the lid down on the toilet so I couldn't get a drink. They kept saying they'd rather have a canary."

Phyllis smiled. "Dude, I hear you. So why were you living with these philistines?"

"Well, it's a complicated story. Guinevere and her partner, a pea-brained philosophy professor, weren't getting along. They yelled at each other night and day, which I found stressful. Finally, he moved out of the apartment, left town, took up with a female student who wrote love poems. Which was fine. He never liked me anyway. He said I gave him everything from hives to jock itch. He even tried to blame me for his tirades. He said I put him on edge. He called me a skulker, an incarnation of the devil. I may be many things, but I'm not Satanic. Guinevere did her best to defend me. Trouble was, after the break-up, she moved to Winnipeg. The company she works for offered her a job there. So she leased a bed-sitter on Portage Avenue. I thought she'd take me with her, but her new landlord wouldn't allow pets. No cats, no dogs, no gerbils. So next thing I know, I'm put up for adoption. One good thing, I didn't have to go through the humiliation of becoming a ward of Hollyland Haven. Guinevere's aunt and uncle came and took me to live with them on Skyline Avenue. I knew I was in trouble when I saw the pink flamingo on the front lawn and the mallard with spinning wings. They'd never owned a cat before. They thought they could lay down rules and regulations. Everyone knows you can't regulate cats. The most you can do is offer suggestions. You can pass edicts till you're blue in the face, but enforcing them is another matter.

"The sad part was that Guinevere cried her eyes out when her aunt and uncle came for me and put me in their car. I wasn't too cheerful myself. I was afraid I might never see her again. It sounded like she was leaving for good and I had no way of getting to Winnipeg. On top of that, I missed the waterfront, the boats, the gulls, the smell of fish. I missed my two old Burmese buddies, Bronco and Grimsby, who lived across the Bayview courtyard, a floor above me. We used to sit on our balconies and make faces at each other. Summer nights, we stayed up late, serenading the neighbourhood. Guinevere's next-door neighbour, Mrs Agrippa, would come out on her balcony and tell us if we didn't shut up, she'd phone the superintendent. I was heartbroken to see those good times come to an end."

Phyllis nodded. "Like I said, dude, I hear you. But if Guinevere lives in Winnipeg, why bother trekking all the way down to Bayview Apartments on Lake Street? Surely not just to see Bonzo and Grimshaw, or whoever."

"Well, yes. What better reason? And to see if by any chance Guinevere has come home. I have a feeling about this. An inkling. A premonition. I see her in dreams. I hear her calling me. I don't see or hear anyone else, only Guinevere."

"So you're hiking on a hunch, dude? Or are you planning a travel book? *Rambles with Rufus*. Sounds harebrained to me. I used to live in a library, and Robert Louis Stevenson's *Travels with a Donkey* has already been done. So has Eric Newby's *A Short Walk in the Hindu Kush*. I just hope that what happened to Robert Falcon Scott at the South Pole doesn't happen to you on Red River Road. I also hope you're not looking for recruits."

Her in-your-face literary references made my head

swim. I also sensed I was being mocked. Rather than let on I didn't know what she was talking about, I said, "No, I'm not looking for recruits. I'm not setting out to climb Mount Everest or swim the English Channel. This is strictly a solo mission, impossible though it may be. I'm going back to the Bayview Apartments on Lake Street to see Guinevere."

"Ah, yes, the fair Guinevere. Wife of King Arthur, but with hinges on her heels for Sir Lancelot. Well, I wish you luck, dude. Maybe someday when you're on your way back to Skyline Avenue, we'll meet again. I'll keep an eye out for you. In the meantime, as Dick Whittington said to his cat, 'Godspeed, bon voyage,' and all that."

Another reason my hike took me so long was that I didn't walk in snow, sleet or slush. Or if it was too windy. Or if I wasn't feeling well. Especially once the cold weather set in. That would have been reckless. Granted, I had no choice but to traverse a divided highway, a dozen busy intersections, a hundred fenced back yards full of dogs. There were school playgrounds, crowded during the week, and church parking lots, crowded on Sundays. Were I to do it again, I might set off in April rather than October. I can see now why sensible folk travel in summer and stay home by the fire in winter. However, I don't claim to be sensible.

Nor do I put much stock in omens, good or bad. The day I started out, Thanksgiving Monday, a flock of ravens followed me from Skyline Avenue to Sherwood Drive. It was the same mob of shifty-eyed vultures that hangs out at the Jumbo Gardens

Community Centre, where they perch on BFI dumpsters and croak at you like gallows birds. I feel about them the way Guinevere's philosophy professor felt about me. Talk about incarnations of the devil.

Because of the ravens, I almost lost my nerve. They made me aware of how alone I was, without family, without friends. The more I thought about it, the more tempted I was to turn back. And I might have, had not some stronger, magnetic, migratory force taken hold of me and pulled me southward.

As dusk fell that evening and lights came on in people's houses, I noticed cats looking out their windows at me. On their faces I saw distrust, suspicion. I envied them, safe indoors on this autumn evening, surrounded by caring family, awaiting supper. I would have given anything to hear Guinevere's voice, to feel her hand on my head. Instead, I heard traffic, police sirens, dogs barking. As though that was't bad enough, I suddenly realized I'd lost my lucky flea collar, the one Guinevere had given me, with my name on it. It must have popped loose while I was cavorting in the wild mint. Either that, or light-fingered Phyllis had slipped it off my neck while I was otherwise occupied.

TWO
An Evening with Queenie and Priapus

I spent that first night in a draughty old garden shed on Hawthorne Drive. If offered protection from the elements and I was able to curl up on a sack of peat moss. Though I was warm enough, and not very hungry, the thin walls of the shed rattled in the wind and kept me awake half the night. Which may have been a good thing, because at first light a small brown mouse scampered in and I had him for breakfast. There was no stalking or hunting involved, as he ran right in, and before he could put on the brakes and run back out, I pounced. There's nothing as tasty as fresh mouse, especially after a diet of store-bought cat food, which I fear is made mostly of ground-up dogfish.

I slept late and didn't get an early start. Even so, traffic was heavy. People were on their way to work after a long weekend. They let their horns do the talking. So I moved off the main drag and tried side streets. This meant more fenced yards, which meant more Rottweilers, and more women yelling at you to stay out of their damned gardens. But at least there were trees to climb in case of danger. It occurred to me that what I should do, being a nocturnal creature, was travel at night. The only difficulty would be finding safe refuge during the daylight hours and avoiding predators, such as owls and alley cats, which come out after dark and either swoop down on you or challenge you to fisticuffs.

Though the weather was fine, I made little progress that day. By evening, when hunger and thirst, those two bugbears of long-distance trekkers, began to make their presence felt, I found myself at the corner of Piccadilly Avenue and Walkover Street. As darkness fell, I stumbled upon a tipped-over garbage can and was able to pick out a few choice morsels for my supper. There was a leg of lamb with meat still on the bone, and the remains of a mouldy plum duff. I found the latter filling, but a tad spicy. I suspected a dog had knocked over the garbage can and been scared off before consuming the best bits. While I feasted, two jealous crows sat on telephone wires overhead and berated me. They made a terrible din and seemed determined to disrupt my meal. Had they been friends, you might have thought they were trying to warn me about something. So intent was I on consuming everything in sight that I ate more than I should have, and much too quickly. With the result that by the time I'd finished, and located a hiding place in a child's abandoned tree house, I was feeling decidedly unwell. I wondered if there'd been too much fungus on the plum duff, or too much mint jelly on the mutton. I also experienced an aftertaste of horseradish. Perhaps that's what the crows were trying to warn me about. Perhaps that's why the delinquent dog had fled.

Things would get worse before they got better. In fact, it was one of the worst nights of my life. It ranked right up there with the night I spent at Hollyland Haven a few years ago, after undergoing what Guinevere and her Kantian paramour referred to as "alterations." Talk about discomfort. I'd have to say, though, that my night in the tree house equalled my first night on Skyline Avenue with Guinevere's aunt and uncle. Besides bloat, I experienced teeth-chattering chills. Being alone when you're sick is no fun, especially at night, in a draughty old tree house.

Next day, I slept till noon. When I got up, a voice in my head kept saying, "It's not too late to turn back, Rufus. They probably haven't missed you yet." But I didn't turn back. I climbed down out of the tree house and pressed on, despite nausea and aching joints. I walked slowly, with frequent stops under hedges to catch my breath, so that it was mid-afternoon before I reached Dublin Avenue. I felt dizzy and cold, then dizzy and hot, then just dizzy. It reminded me of the time a few years ago when Guinevere's slimy sophist (she called him Aristotle when she was mad at him) gave me some tainted catnip.

I didn't cross the Expressway until after dark. It was easier to traverse four lanes of traffic when you could see headlights. I scampered across to the median, took a careful look, then ran like the wind to the ditch on the far side. Just as I jumped to safety in the tall grass, a transport truck roared by, trailing clouds of dust and diesel fumes. Its slipstream was like a tornado. When it had passed, I climbed up out of the ditch and made a beeline for Blucher Avenue. Trudging along through burrs and bracken, keeping an eye open for a place to spend the night, I spotted a lumpy grey female cat sitting on what I thought at first was a stump, but which turned out to be a pile of bricks, left over from some prehistoric demolition. I expected this ratty old grimalkin, whose whiskers were bent and broken, to order me off her estate. I expected her to shout, "This is restricted land! Posted territory. My private game preserve. So unless you're just passing through, don't even think about stopping."

Surprisingly, she didn't say that. She didn't say anything. All she did was size me up. In the gloom, I couldn't see what colour her eyes were, only that they gleamed when she turned her head toward a distant street lamp. Finally she said, "I watched you cross the Expressway, Bumpkin. Either you have a death wish or you lack the brains God gave grasshoppers. You obviously aren't experienced with four-lane highways. I'm surprised you're not lying out there, flat as a pancake."

Though what she said was true, I was stung by her criticism. "Well, I made it, didn't I?"

"By luck, not skill. Your first time away from home, Sonny? What's your name?"

"Rufus. What's yours?"

"I have several. At the moment, I'm Queenie. Also Annabel. The first family I ever lived with called me Bernadette. After that I was Clementine. Lately I answer to Old Shrew, because of the sour mood I'm in."

She did seem out of sorts, cantankerous, menopausal. To be polite, I said, "And why are you in a sour mood, Queenie?"

She sighed, stretched, looked down at me. "When you get to be my age, you don't need a reason. You just are. Little aches and pains. Your eyesight isn't what it used to be. Your teeth hurt. You can't hear mice in the grass. You can't jump like you used to, or stand up to impudent toms. Your temper gets frayed. You lose patience. Old age is no fun. Your favourite foods are tasteless. The slowest moth is too fast. I'd rather be young. My fur has lost its sheen. I only come out after dark, when folks can't see me. Someday, if you learn how to cross highways properly, you'll know what I mean. So where are you from and where are you headed?"

"I'm from Skyline Avenue and I'm headed for the Bayview Apartments on Lake Street. It's where I used to live, with a lady named Guinevere and her philandering boyfriend, Aristotle. She moved to Winnipeg and gave me to her aunt and uncle. Things didn't work out."

"So you're headed home?"

"I'm headed home."

"Except, if I heard you right, Guinevere no longer lives on Lake Street. So I don't quite see the logic of your plan."

"My plan has no logic. It's just something I must do."

"That's quite a jaunt. Seems to me you should have stayed on Skyline Avenue. There's many a cat who'd call you crazy, giving up the good life for a walk on the wild side. And for what? To satisfy some momentary urge."

"It's no momentary urge. I've thought it over."

"If you thought it over the way you cross highways, I'd say you've blundered. But the grass is always greener, isn't it? Ah, the impetuosity of youth. Always doing things on the spur of the moment. Failing to consider consequences. No wonder Hollyland Haven is full."

This wasn't talk I needed to hear, and I started to turn away. It was then that I understood why Queenie was perched on a pile of bricks. The grass was so tall in this vacant lot, this former warehouse site, that from ground level you couldn't see a thing. I'd taken only a few faltering steps when Queenie said, "If you're looking for Red River Road, Bumpkin, you're headed in the wrong direction. If I were you, I'd find shelter for the night. You look a little shaky."

"I'm not shaky. I'm fine."

"Sure you are. I don't much cotton to shaky cats, but in your case, I'll make an exception. At the moment, I'm living with two spinster ladies over on Picton Avenue. They allow me the attic of their house in exchange for rodent control. It's quiet and I have my own entrance. Nothing lavish. No feather beds. No maid service, but it beats living on the street. My toothless old pal Priapus, from Sequoia Drive, sometimes drops in for a chat. I think you'd like him. He's made a career out of not being shaky too. He's the interracial product of a blue Burmese and a yellow Persian, so he's seen his share of bigotry. In his prime, besides tutoring me, he once walked from Glengary Drive to Hastings Place. In mid-summer, mind you. Still, he might give you pointers."

"I don't need pointers, Queenie. And I have a long way to go, so I really should push on. Not that I don't appreciate the offer."

"Suit yourself, Charles."

"Charles?"

"Charles Lindbergh. He had a long way to go too. Have you taken a close look at the sky lately? There's a big storm coming. A deluge. A torrential downpour. You'll think you're in the Amazon rainforest. I feel it in my bones."

As though to emphasize her words, the first raindrops fell. Moments later, there was a rumble of thunder and a gust of wind. After a little rethinking, I decided to accept her invitation. I said, "Queenie, I've changed my mind. You talked me into it. Your attic and your friend Priapus intrigue me. As I've no desire to be caught in the rain, why don't you lead the way?"

She jumped down off her pile of bricks, started through the tall grass, waving her tail. It was like being on safari. Over her shoulder she said, "Bumpkin, you remind me of a rooster I once knew. His name was Rafe. He was unorthodox, not to say eccentric. Didn't fit the mould. Didn't play by the rules. Didn't know what was expected of him. He used to crow at all hours of the day or night. Never the same time twice, and never first thing in the morning. We told him, 'Rafe, you don't understand what's expected of you. You were put on this earth to crow at daybreak. Your behaviour confuses people.' But he just didn't get it. He crowed at noon, midnight, or three o'clock in the morning. He was either psychotic, or too imaginative for his own good. Whenever the spirit moved him, he crowed. People said, 'Rafe, get with the program.' But he never did. He had a mind of his own, like you. I figure he was either a genius or a nut case."

Queenie's snug loft was indeed a good place to be on a rainy October night. It was in the attic of the last house on Picton Avenue, around the corner from

Blucher Crescent. At first glance, you might have expected to see a witch emerge from the shrubbery and tempt you with gingerbread. But there were no witches. Only grotesque trees, waving in the wind, and lighted windows on the ground floor. There was a rickety fire escape leading to a door under the eaves, and it was up this ancient ladder, with half its rungs missing, that Queenie and I scrambled. No sooner had we reached the top than the rain started coming down in torrents. I wondered at first how we'd gain entrance, until I saw that the door lacked a section of lower panel, which left a hole big enough for a cat to squeeze through. Inside, just as Queenie had promised, it was warm and dry. It would have been quiet too, except for the drumming rain. On planks laid across rafters there were old lamps, books, broken suitcases, cartons of clothing, a dusty guitar, a cracked mandolin. I never did see Queenie's spinster landladies, but I heard their voices as they rattled around down below, arguing over what to have for supper. As they were both deaf, they had the stereo turned up loud. So whether we wanted to or not, we listened to Beethoven's Pastoral Symphony. This was pleasant enough accompaniment to the rain, as well as to the rattle of pots and pans. We could soon smell cutlets frying. Which was unusual, according to Queenie. She said that most nights the two old ladies settled for Lean Cuisine. I must say, the smell of frying meat, which under normal circumstances might have made my mouth water, did nothing for me that evening, as I was still suffering from my touch of food poisoning.

I'm not sure what time Queenie's friend Priapus arrived. I was reclining in a box of quilts, perfectly relaxed, listening to the rain and the racket of Beethoven's thunderstorm, when I heard an older voice address Queenie as "Mademoiselle Golightly." Stealthy Priapus had tiptoed in without fanfare, and when I looked up, I saw him giving me the once-over. He was a damp, tiger-striped shorthair, with scars on his face and a crooked tail. Actually, the end of his tail was missing, as were the tips of his ears. When he walked he limped.

"This is Rufus," Queenie informed him. "A callow friend of mine. Still wet behind the ears, as you are too, but for different reasons. He's on an expedition to Lake Street."

Priapus raised his eyebrows, shook his head. "Lake Street? That's a haul this time of year. I wish him luck."

"He pines for fickle Guinevere, who gave him to her aunt and uncle on Skyline Avenue."

Priapus nodded knowingly, as though the story were a familiar one. "Ah, yes. The homesick exile. Napoleon on St Helena, longing for Paris. Hannibal in Crete, longing for Carthage. He committed suicide, rather than let the Romans catch him. But that's extreme. I wish you luck, young fellow. I'm surprised you're not wearing a bell. That seems to be the rage these days. If you want to impress the ladies. And I'm sure you do. Sow some wild oats. Cut a wide swath."

I thought I detected a note of scorn. "If I cut a swath, Mr Priapus, it will be a narrow one. I've been altered."

He smiled, flicked his crooked tail. "Welcome to the club. I've been altered too. Still, I look back on my youth fondly. Those were the days. No inkling of old age. Boundless energy. Party all night, sleep all day. But listen, if you can't cut a wide swath, you can still have fun. I'm talking oral history here. Urban legend. A legacy for your grandchildren. Well, no. Not if you've been altered. Still, there's no shame in being altered. I know many an altered cat. Take my friend Hildegarde. She lives with the nuns down at St Joseph's Heritage. I'll give you an introduction. The Sisters are good for a handout, especially in winter. Hildegarde, as you might imagine, is a staunch Catholic cat."

It was entertaining, listening to Priapus and Queenie talk of old times. As young kittens, they'd been part of the same household, in a ramshackle house on Wentworth Crescent. Here, they frolicked, chased each other, got into mischief. Their favourite game was hide-and-seek, played at night, when everyone else was asleep. They used the entire house, upstairs and down, calling to each other, galloping from room to room, until someone would open the door and evict them. Neither remembered what had happened to end these carefree days. Priapus seemed to recall a domestic squabble, after which he'd come home and found Queenie gone and the place occupied by strangers. He'd searched the neighbourhood without success, had finally gone to live in a stable on Castlegreen Drive. In those days, people on Castlegreen Drive kept horses and chickens. He'd survived on rats, and the horses had been grateful to him, because, believe it or not, rodents frightened them.

    I don't remember dozing off, but I did, and slept soundly, except for an unsettling dream about a field of bracken and a busy highway. When I woke up, I was alone in the attic. Queenie was gone, and so was

Priapus. The rain had stopped and there was light in the eastern sky. I might have been miffed at Queenie's desertion, had she not told me the night before that she'd promised to babysit grandchildren while their mother hunted magpies. Downstairs, I could hear the two old spinsters arguing about what to have for breakfast.

And so I climbed down the rickety fire escape, took my bearings, and started off for Windsor Street, which runs right by Hammarskjold High School. It was a cool, grey morning, with an autumnal bite in the air, and as I walked along, hearing the faint ringing of school bells and boys shouting as they threw a football back and forth, I felt pellets of sleet landing on my fur.

*

THREE
Hattie and the Sandsuckers

Where Cherry Lane joins Oak Avenue there's a small green space, a sort of miniature park, with two maple trees, a broken teeter-totter and three dogwood bushes. I arrived there at mid-morning, just as the sun peeped out. I dug a little earth at the base of a tree and was about to continue on my way when I noticed a whiskery old gentleman, in scarf and jacket, sitting all by himself on the one and only park bench. He was just sitting there, looking around at the flitting chickadees, watching a clumsy grey squirrel in the branches overhead. I say clumsy, because the squirrel seemed anything but sure-footed. Sooner or later, I expected to see him come tumbling down. He was snacking on those little winged seed pods that grow on maple trees, eating the seeds and dropping the wings on the old man's hat. I kept thinking that if the squirrel did fall out of the tree, I'd be on him in a flash. What's more tasty than maple-flavoured squirrel?

To me, the old man looked lonely. Whether he was or not, who knows? I may simply have been transferring my own mood to him. But when I saw him move to one end of the bench, as though making room for me, I went closer. In a gruff, but not unfriendly voice, he said, "Hello there, Cat. What are you doing out on such a chilly day?"

I felt like saying, "Chilly? This isn't chilly, old-timer. If you think this is chilly, wait a month." But I didn't say that. Instead, when he patted the bench in an invitational way, I jumped up beside him. He knew better than to touch me, or try to get familiar. I could tell he understood cats. He said, "When my wife Jessie was alive, she once had a cat like you. Same colour. Same eyes. A bit bigger, though. Longer fur. She spoiled him. Called him Big Al, after Al Capone. Said he was a hit man. Said he terrorized the neighbourhood. Could have been your father. My name's Plimsoll, by the way."

So we sat there a while, watching the traffic on Windsor Street. A lady went by, pushing a two-seat stroller with twins in it. She smiled at us, nodded, but didn't say anything. She may have thought Plimsoll and I knew each other. She may have thought, "Well, isn't that quaint? An old geezer and his cat, out for their morning constitutional."

During a lull in the traffic, Plimsoll said, "We sometimes sat on this bench, back when Jessie was still mobile. Or on a bench in Sequoia Place. But finally it got so she didn't know where she was. She'd panic. She'd think we were lost. She'd want me to call a taxi. I'd say, 'It's all right, Jess, I know where we are. I'll get us home. You just stick with me.' One day I told her we should sell the house and move into an apartment. But she was afraid to. I said, 'Jess, the day will come when I can't look after you, or you after me, and we'll need help. We should sell the house and buy a condo.' But she wouldn't. She said, 'What's the rush, Irving? I like it here. I'm accustomed to it. Anyway, we've lots of time. We're both still healthy.' And then she fell down the basement stairs and broke her hip, and by the time that healed, she was in sad shape. Her eyesight went to hell, she caught pleurisy. She'd go days without getting out of bed. I tried to get her into a facility—Dawson Court, Bethammi, Pioneer Ridge—but they were all full. Minimum ten-month waiting list. So finally she ended up in the hospital, and didn't know who I was, or who she was, or what she'd done to deserve all this. I tell you, Cat, it broke my heart to visit her. After all the good years we'd had. All the good times. But I knew. I knew we should have moved to an apartment. I could see it coming. I should have insisted. Jess would have been happier and lived longer. It's ironic, but that's where I live now. Alone, in a subsidized apartment. They won't allow cats or dogs. Not even birds. Only goldfish. So I can't invite you home for lunch. Stupid regulations. I'm surprised they let me keep Jessie's ashes in a vase."

As engrossing as Mr Plimsoll's story was, the squirrel in the maple tree interested me more. Since he wasn't going to fall, I wondered whether I shouldn't just nip up there and snag him. Instead of dining at Irving Plimsoll's subsidized apartment, I'd have lunch right there on the park bench.

I'd swear that squirrel read my mind. He stopped munching seed pods, dropped the last wing on Irving's hat, and took off through the branches, chattering as he went.

Irving stood up, sat down, stood up again. "You look a lot like Jessie's cat. If I didn't know he'd been dead ten years, I'd swear you was him. The sad thing is, after Jess quit recognizing me, didn't know me from a hole in the ground, she still kept asking about Al Capone. She'd say to me, 'Sir, have you seen my cat, Big Al Capone? He went out last night and didn't come back.' And I'd say, 'No Jess, I haven't seen Big Al, but if we wait a while, maybe he'll show up.' Of course he never did. Next day Jess would ask the orderly if he'd seen her cat, and he'd say, 'Yes, ma'am, I saw him out in the garden chasing butterflies. He's very agile for an old cat.' And Jess would say, "Old? Big Al's not old. I got him as a kitten. If anything ever happened to him, I don't know what I'd do. Ever since I lost my husband, he's all I've got left.' And I'd be right there, in her room, listening, and she'd have no idea who I was. Once she asked me if I was on the campaign trail and did I want her vote. She said my face looked familiar from posters and TV. 'But I won't vote for you,' she'd say. 'Not unless you find my cat and bring him home. He's a good cat, a clean cat, who eats what I feed him and never scratches. But like most men, he's got the wanderlust. Like my late husband, who used to disappear for days on end and then come back, expecting forgiveness. Until the day he didn't come back. I don't know what became of him. Maybe he went home to his mother. Come to think of it, I believe I read his obituary in the newspaper. It said he was married to someone else. Someone I didn't know. I phoned the paper and told them they'd made a mistake.'"

The lady with the two-seat stroller went by again, walking faster, into the wind. Both babies were wailing. Their mother seemed oblivious to their distress. She was more interested in Plimsoll. She may have wondered about his sanity. He was, after all, sitting on a park bench, talking animatedly to a cat. As she hurried by, she shook her head, as though now she'd seen everything. Plimsoll stood up, squared his shoulders, started walking in the opposite direction. Toward his subsidized apartment, no doubt. Under other circumstances, I might have followed him, but that day I didn't.

I spent the early part of the afternoon sauntering down Algonquin Avenue. Or should I say down the lane between Algonquin and Kenogami. At the corner of Sydney Street, on the front steps of a stucco house surrounded by hawthorn hedges, I saw a pert young orange shorthair sunning herself. Normally, when I see cats on people's front steps, I give them a wide berth. More often than not, they prove to be territorial. If you so much as glance in their direction, they growl. If you slow down, they tell you to keep moving. I guess they're afraid you might try to horn in. They can be quite insensitive. "Excuse me, but this house is taken, Buster. It has room for only one cat, and that's me."

But this orange cat didn't say that. Her eyes were closed and I thought at first she hadn't noticed me. But as I passed by she called out, "Are we like totally stuck-up today? No time for chit-chat?"

I stopped, took a closer look. Was she offering sarcasm or friendship? It was hard to tell. She wore a designer flea collar. Judging by her glossy coat, she was well looked after. Probably pampered. On the door behind her hung a sign: "Beware of Attack Cat." She didn't look much like an attack cat, nor, when she spoke, did she sound much like one. "Hi, sailor," she said, with mock seductiveness. "My name is Hortense. New in town?"

"Just passing through. On my way to Lake Street."

"And, like, freedom?"

"I beg your pardon?"

"Hearing not so good? I said, 'and, like, freedom?' You could be a fugitive. Or a bounty hunter. These days, who can tell? Why not sit and chew the fat? Like, tell me your life story. Know what I'm saying? Unless of course you're late for an appointment."

"No, I'm not late. I have all the time in the world."

"I can't offer you anything. No root, no catnip. I'm not allowed visitors. Know what I'm saying? I'm out here while the house is being, like, fumigated. Or vacuumed. Or some damn thing. Gives me the jimjams. Sets my teeth on edge. Especially the vacuum sweeper. Know what I'm saying? You'd think I'd be used to it by now, but I'm not. I go crazy. I'm liable to climb the curtains and kick heirlooms off the mantelpiece. So I'm out here till things calm down. Twice a year, spring and fall. Screw that, right? My keepers, the Sandsuckers, are neatness freaks. Like, show me a fastidious cat and I'll show you a psychopath. Know what I'm saying? Probably not. So tell me, why Lake Street?"

"It's a long story. Did you say Sandsuckers?"

"That's what I call them. It's not their real name. So, is your story extra long? If it is, why not give me the abridged version. Or if it's also ugly, save your breath, right?"

"I'm on a sort of pilgrimage."

"A pilgrimage? No shit. I thought people went on pilgrimages in April. Shows how much I know. The furthest I've ever been is Hollyland Haven. That's an animal shelter for transients, right? Mine's a long story too. A sordid blast from the past. What's your name?"

"Rufus."

"Rufus? Cool. I once had an uncle named Rufus. Bit of a loser. Fell off the jackknife bridge one foggy night. No more pilgrimages for Uncle Rufus. Like I said, my name's Hortense. A pukey name for a cat, right? I'm like totally freaked every time I hear it. It means 'female horticulturalist' in Latin. Like, who cares? Give me a break, right? They call me Hattie, for short. Which isn't so bad."

So I went and sat with Hattie on the front steps of her stucco house. It was quite pleasant there, out of the wind, hidden by hedges. When the sun poked out from behind the overcast, we could feel its warmth on our fur. But when clouds moved in, there was a chill in the air. Hattie said, "No denying it, right? Days are shrinking, nights getting longer. As the old Dutch poet says, 'Winter is a-coomin' in, All sing Goddamm!'"

With no prompting from me, other than my observation that cats, like snakes, thrive on sunshine, Hattie spoke of her stay at Hollyland Haven. While waiting to be adopted, she'd enjoyed sunning herself in the enclosure every afternoon, climbing into the lower branches of a fir tree, whose resinous perfume she found mildly arousing. She said she had a friend there, a young Burmese named Quigley, for whom she felt sorry, because Quigley had no front claws. Which meant he was unable to climb trees or defend himself. To compensate, he'd become adept at jumping and biting.

"It was totally cool at Hollyland, right? Quiet. Relaxing. We ate well, slept a lot, sat around talking.

Oh, there were a few malcontents. There always are, right? Spiteful gossips. Always needing psychoanalysis, or tranquilizers, or some damn thing. Right? The misfits were like, segregated? As were the dogs. Thank God there were no horses. Like, not while I was there? Although we did have a pot-bellied pig and a cool parrot. The pig stayed outdoors in all weather. Rain, snow, hurricanes. Know what I'm saying? He didn't care. Give him a mud puddle and some plastic toys and he was happy. The parrot knew like three hundred words and called everybody Pussy. Even the staff. He was like, 'Pussy, I love what you've done with your hair.' Or, 'Pussy, your deodorant's not working.' It's funny, but when I was finally adopted by the Sandsuckers and came to live here, I wondered if I'd turned my back on a good thing. Of course I hadn't. This is much better, right? Still, sometimes I miss the old gang. Know what I'm saying, Rufus? Probably not."

Which made me smile. "Yes, Hattie. I know exactly what you're saying."

She shook her head vigorously, as though she'd been swimming. "Damn these ear mites. You ever have ear mites, Rufus? The scourge of catdom. That and fleas. Which is why I wear this stupid flea collar, right? It has my name on it. My calico friend next door, Melanie, has a tattoo under her tail and a microchip implanted in her belly. Can you imagine? She's electronically challenged. The question is, like, *why*?"

I couldn't think of an answer, so I said nothing. It occurred to me, though, that I should soon be on my way. The day was wearing on and there was an unmistakable nip in the air. I wouldn't have been surprised to see snowflakes. Besides, Hortense was beginning to bore me ever so slightly. To be truthful, I wasn't much interested in hearing about her residency at Hollyland Haven. I had my own itinerary to focus on.

Just as I was about to take my leave, Hattie said, "You know what I think, Rufus? I think you need a cool pedigree name, right? To make it in this world, you have to appear distinguished. So from now on, when anyone asks your name, tell them it's Red Rufus from Minch. When I was at Hollyland Haven, that's what we did to pass the time. Gave each other pedigree names. I was Macaboy Macebearer. That got people's attention. The pig was Purdah Portcullis. The parrot was Purselane the Purveyor. Quigley was Jiggery-Pokery III. Cool names with character, right? See what I'm saying? Probably not."

Luckily, I was saved from having to answer, because at that moment the door flew open and a short, fat, bald man came storming out with a broom in his hands. Not a vacuum sweeper, but a plain, old-fashioned broom. I wasn't sure what his intentions were, nor did I hang around to find out. "Scat!" he yelled, waving the broom like a hockey stick. So that's what I did. Red Rufus from Minch scatted. I'm not sure, but I think I heard Hattie giggle. Mr Sandsucker, or whatever his name was, said to her, "Damn strays! Was that cat bothering you, Hortense?"

I didn't hear her answer, because by then I was through the hawthorn hedge and heading for Beresford Street. I didn't totally run, but I didn't, like, take my time either. Know what I'm saying?

*

FOUR
Just Can't Wait to Get on the Road Again

I've often wondered how things might have turned out had I kept going toward Beresford Street instead of branching off at Windemere. How is one to judge in hindsight, let alone foretell, the consequences of one's choices? You could spend a lifetime asking yourself, "What if . . . ?"

After leaving Hattie and Mr Sandsucker on their doorstep, I trudged along rather dispiritedly. The grey October skies and nasty wind didn't help. Sometime during the afternoon I developed hiccups. They worsened with the approach of evening. I was hungry, yet not hungry. There was a ringing in my ears. My paws hurt. I felt stiff, sore, tense. Part of it was from having to keep a sharp lookout for trouble. Not just for traffic, but for untethered dogs, territorial cats and urchins throwing crabapples at me. There was also the concern of finding a safe place to spend the night.

Halfway along Windemere Avenue, walking slowly, I realized I was being observed by a lady wearing a house dress and babushka. She was standing on her front steps, within arm's reach of a candleberry tree, filling a phallic-shaped bird feeder. No harm in that. I'm all for feeding the birds. I only wish someone would put out tidbits for migratory cats. In spite of myself, I shivered. I suppose I made a pitiful sight, but what could I do? The shivering was involuntary. I knew my feet had been dragging. I knew I'd been looking back over my shoulder. My energy was at a low ebb. It had been one of those days.

While I was thus self-absorbed, the woman in the babushka came down her sidewalk and approached me. At first, I thought she had a destination in mind. Which is why I didn't get out of her way. The next thing I knew, she'd picked me up, put me under her arm, and was carrying me toward her house. I was pretty sure I could smell liquor on her breath. Normally, I'd have made an effort to escape. But there was something about this woman, about the feel of her bony hip and the firmness of her hands, that reassured me. She said, "You're not from around here, are you?" It was more a statement of fact than a question. Evidently she knew the neighbourhood cats by sight. I wondered whether she thought I was a threat to her birds. "You look like you're all alone, me bucko. I don't run a flophouse, nor a boarding house, nor a brothel, but I know a welfare case when I see one."

I wasn't sure what she meant, but as I sensed no hostility, I allowed myself to be carried indoors. There were three rooms and not much furniture. Two chairs, a table, a sagging couch and a floor lamp. This wasn't at all like Guinevere's Bayview apartment. Or like my home on Skyline Avenue. Compared to the babushka lady's digs, those places had been palatial. Here, by contrast, in this simple cottage on Windemere Avenue, the bedroom looked like a monk's cell. The stove and fridge were prehistoric.

And yet, there was something comforting about these bare rooms, on whose walls hung K-Mart prints of full-rigged schooners. I felt at ease, unafraid. To my surprise, the babushka lady, humming to herself, placed me on the kitchen table. Any time I'd tried to claim this privilege on Skyline Avenue, I'd been threatened with decapitation. I was so confused I began washing my tail, which is something I do when I'm not sure what's expected of me.

As with old Mr Plimsoll earlier in the day, the babushka lady was soon telling me the story of her life. I began to wonder what quality I had that inspired strangers to bare their souls. Were people really that lonely? Were they so desperate for a listener that they confided in cats? First off, she said her name was Minnie and she was a displaced Nova Scotian. She'd been born in Antigonish, had lived all her life on Chedabucto Bay, a mile from Cape Canso. But the year she turned forty, tragedy had struck. Her husband and son had both drowned when a terrible winter storm sank their fishing boat off Cape St. Mary. Not only that, her aged parents, one blind, the other deaf, had died within a week of each other. Which was a blessing for the two of them, she supposed. In his younger days, prior to being impeached for embezzling municipal funds, her father had been mayor of Antigonish. (Guinevere, who loved myths, once told me that Antigone was the daughter of Oedipus.) And so Minnie had come west to live with her divorced sister, Muriel. They'd been reasonably happy together on Windemere Avenue, working as housemaids, taking in laundry, selling baked goods door to door. Until one summer Muriel ran off to Alberta with a long-distance Trimac trucker, saying she deemed this her final chance for happiness. Minnie might have gone back to Nova Scotia, if she'd had the train fare, but she didn't, and damned if she'd ride the bus all that way.

She said she dabbled in astrology. Not only dabbled in it, but took it very seriously. She was a Sagittarius, and her horoscope showed bleak prospects. She said that Mars and Saturn had been in Virgo the night her son and husband drowned. They were in the same configuration now, and would remain there for the next two years. Which was why she didn't go out much and wasn't looking forward to the future. She said she'd been to see an occultist recently, who had read the Tarot cards and perceived a cemetery, a hospital with bars on the windows, and a burning schoolhouse. "What does it mean, me bucko? It means I should get me to a nunnery."

Humming to herself, she rattled through her empty cupboards, looking for something to eat. She opened the fridge, and I could see there wasn't much in there either. A loaf of bread, a dozen eggs, three bottles of Catawba. "I don't do much cooking these days, me bucko," she said. "Not since Muriel up and left. I thought I had a tin of bully beef here somewhere. I guess I don't. Maybe I ate it. I have Kraft Dinner, but any cat I ever owned, and I've owned a few, turned up their nose at Kraft Dinner. I once had a pair of Siamese, Shiva and Shalom, who ate nothing but cod cheeks. Tonight, me bucko, for you and me, it looks like Kraft Dinner."

As I sat there, waiting for my macaroni and listening to her talk, it occurred to me that while gracious Guinevere had been very hands-on, giving me frequent strokings (unlike her boorish boyfriend, Aristotle, who touched me only with a rolled-up newspaper), Minnie tended to be less tactile. She may have thought I had an aversion to being touched. Which I didn't. At that moment, I could have used a hug and some fondling.

"At least you ain't emaciated," she observed. "Nor battle-scarred. Not like them herring-choker cats. So wherever you come from, you've done well. I can see by your eyes you don't trust me, though. Which is good. These days, you can't be too careful. I've heard of hungry immigrants eating domestic cat."

Eventually, she poured out two bowls of Kraft Dinner, sprinkled on some dried parsley, sat down at the table. "Bon appétit," she said, pushing one bowl toward me and dipping into the other with a spoon. I crouched, sniffed, watched steam rising. Minnie was half finished her meal and on her second glass of Catawba before my dinner was cool enough to eat. At which point I showed her I was one cat who didn't turn up his nose at Kraft Dinner. It wasn't my favourite food (give me filet mignon or twitching sparrow any day), but the cheesy noodles slid down easily. Sipping her third glass of Catawba, Minnie said, "Just because you ain't falling-down hungry don't mean you can't use a square meal. Sometimes I take the edge off with a glass of this here turpentine. It scrambles your brains but tastes better than Lavoris."

As talkative as Minnie had been before we ate, after four glasses of wine and two cigarettes, she lay back in her chair, put her feet up, and dozed off. I think she was unaccustomed to entertaining dinner guests. And so I climbed into the remaining chair and made myself comfortable. I couldn't help thinking about Guinevere, and how we used to sit on her balcony after supper and read the newspaper together. We enjoyed each other's company. Unlike her boyfriend, I didn't come home at all hours, covered in lipstick, walking bowlegged, reeking of cheap perfume.

Listening to Minnie's maternal snores, I thought about my own late mother. I suspect this might have been because during the evening, Minnie had mentioned hers. The last time I saw Mama, she looked old and tired. Her fur was the colour of Minnie's faded wallpaper. She wanted to know where I'd been, what I'd been doing. She'd had no news of my siblings either. She said it saddened her when one of her children, after being away for weeks, or months (or, in my brother Bobby's case, two years), would suddenly appear at some social event. "Where have you been?" she'd ask. "Why didn't you send word? You absent yourself, then show up out of nowhere. It's unconscionable."

I remember once trying to tell her that such meanderings were necessary, so that the gene pool didn't stagnate. New blood was a hedge against inbreeding, against insanity, against extinction. But Mama said I was talking through my hat.

By the same token, she was appalled at how many kittens her daughters had borne out of wedlock. These were grandchildren she refused to acknowledge. Better, she said, to settle in with a nice family and be appreciated as a pet, than to roam the streets like a harlot or live in a cat colony. Our most serious disagreement concerned the bohemian lifestyle of my stepsister Imogene. One year she had three litters with three different husbands, none of whom she lived with for more than a week. Mama thought this disgraceful. I annoyed her by saying I saw nothing wrong with it. That's how cats are, I said. People too.

Mama was also intolerant of my cousin Quentin's effeminate mannerisms. She criticized his daintiness, his affinity for anything made of silk. She rolled her eyes at the way he walked. She'd say to him, "Quentin, for God's sake, stop mincing. Go roll in the mud. Eat some catnip. You look ridiculous. You'll have the neighbours talking."

Had she been able to, Mama would have arranged the marriages of all her offspring. She orchestrated the union between my sister Ramona and a debonair tom named Jerome, whom she considered the perfect mate. Little did she know what a lecher he was, or that he'd break Ramona's heart. I attended their nuptials, which took place in a field of buttercups behind Grandview arena. First off, the bride had to be sent for, because she'd marked her mental calendar for the following night. No sooner had things got under way than we were dispersed by a gang of children chasing fireflies. Then when the dust settled and we reconvened, the groom was nowhere to be found. Later he was, though. Behind a saxifrage bush, in the arms of a tortie-tabby from Perth Crescent.

What finally snapped me out of this genealogical, macaroni-induced reverie was Minnie talking in her sleep. I couldn't tell what she was saying, or who she was addressing, but she seemed to be speaking in Mama's voice. Which, for reasons that I can't begin to explain, made me feel warm and fuzzy. Then very drowsy. So I curled up with my tail over my nose, and while I slept, I dreamed. In the dream, Mama and I were walking through a ruined city. Or if not a ruined city, then slums. Apparently there had been an earthquake. Buildings had crumbled, streets were torn up. Grass was growing through the pavement. Mama seemed to know where she was going, and was not in the least perturbed when Minnie joined us. We came to a fetid swamp, where skeletal trees were festooned with Spanish moss. I was struggling to keep up, slowed down by heat, flies and wet feet. Vivid flowers flashed before my eyes. (Who says cats don't dream in colour?) Pungent smells assailed my nostrils: cedar, garlic, vandalroot. But what scared me was the thought of snakes. The more I worried about stepping on a snake, the further behind I got. Finally I called out to Mama and Minnie, begged them to wait for me. By now they were out of sight and I could hear them laughing. Splashing through mud up to my knees, completely disoriented, I wondered why they were being so cruel. At the same time, their fading laughter was my homing beacon. I knew if that died, so would I.

I awoke with a start, beset by vague fears, trying to remember what Minnie had said about hungry immigrants eating domestic cats. Was she herself an immigrant? That might explain her eagerness to nourish me. I looked for her, but she wasn't in her chair. As I headed for the door, I saw her in her bedroom, lying down, smoking a cigarette. She must have heard me, because a moment later she came shuffling out in her slippers and bathrobe. "I figured sooner or later you'd need a breath of fresh air. By the bye, me bucko, you were meowing in your sleep. Like you were in pain. Kept me awake. Maybe them noodles was expired. I feel a bit queasy myself."

Lighting a fresh cigarette, holding the door open for me, she recoiled at the rush of cold air. "Now don't you be long out there, me bucko. Catch your death of pneumonia, and me too. That's all we bloody need."

I did not return. I hoped Minnie wouldn't stand there all night waiting for me. No doubt she felt abandoned. First by her son and husband, then by her sister Muriel, and now by me, an itinerant cat to whom she'd offered hospitality. Did she consider me ungrateful? Probably. How long, I wondered, might I have stayed with her, had I not felt compelled to leave? It wasn't just the booze, the bare cupboards, and the Kraft Dinner. I'm not sure what it was. It might have been Minnie herself. Thinking of sweet Guinevere, I set off resolutely into that chilly grey October dawn. As they say in trekking parlance, I hit the trail. It seemed necessary. Still, I wonder how much difference a tin or two of Whiskas would have made. Poor Minnie. Life is rough when you're alone. Maybe all we can hope for is someone to care for us when we're old. I couldn't help wondering, as I started toward Marlborough Street, how much happier Muriel was, out in Alberta with her long-distance Trimac trucker. I know how she felt. I know what made her flee. I understand her restlessness. As Willie Nelson has been known to say: "I just can't wait to get on the road again."

*

FIVE
Christmas with Theo
and His Yellow Pine Coffin

All morning, as cold mist swirled on the boulevards and hung from trees in tendrils, I pressed on toward Marlborough Street. Crossing Rockwood, I ran a veritable gauntlet of shifty-eyed alley cats, who seemed to have congregated, for what illicit purpose I couldn't imagine, along the leaf-choked curbstones. Watching me go by, they bared their yellow fangs, humped their backs, hissed offensively. I had the feeling there was some kind of turf war in progress. It was like a scene from a bad western movie, or *Lawrence of Arabia*, with the good guys and bad guys squared off, facing each other, bristling with bravado. I kept looking for Peter O'Toole, or a five-star sheriff in chaps and a white hat. Or maybe this was some kind of urban stand-off, as in *West Side Story*. Strutting rights might have been at stake. Or access to a patch of wild juniper. I really didn't care. All I wanted to do was pass by without insult or altercation. Without anyone asking me where I was going, then telling me I was stupid to attempt such a feat at this time of year. I could hear them saying, "No cat in his right mind, except maybe a snow leopard, would plan a winter expedition. You obviously haven't thought this through. What happens if you get caught in a blizzard? How do you propose to survive in cold weather? You must be crazy. Better you should join us."

So I ignored the curled lips, flattened ears and lashing tails. If a territorial dispute was in progress, I wanted no part of it. I was, after all, as I'd been telling people, only passing through. I had problems enough of my own.

I walked until noon, when a chilly rain began to fall. If there's one thing I can't stand, it's wet fur. It gives me the heebie-jeebies. I feel clammy, inside and out. My joints ache, my ears twitch. If I stay out in the rain too long, I get dizzy. Of course, I'm exaggerating, but still, there's nothing so bedraggled and smelly as a wet cat. Unless it's a wet dog. Horses and cows are different. They can stand out in the rain all day. Cats can't.

And so as I walked, I kept an eye open for suitable shelter. Oddly enough, it wasn't my eye that spotted a likely place, it was my nose. A block or two from the north end of Hodge Street, within sight of St Elmo's Anglican Church, I detected the enticing scent of fresh-cut cedar. This is a smell I adore. It draws me like perfume. If I were to detect barbecued steak in the north, smoked salmon in the east, roast turkey in the south and cedar in the west, I'd head straight for the setting sun.

The delicious aroma, I soon discovered, was coming from a sort of garage or workshop at the upper end of Cornwall Avenue. The house in the front yard wasn't much to look at, but you could see that someone had spent time beautifying the garage. It was painted forest green with white curlicues and had ornately carved wooden animals nailed to its exterior walls: foxes, elk, otters, bobcats. In the sleety afternoon light, its windows glowed cheerily. The planet wasn't deserted after all. I looked for a smoking chimney, as evidence of a stove or fireplace, but there was none. Not until later, when I was warm and snug inside with Mr Godyke, did I discover that he relied on electric heat. He said that this was both an advantage and a disadvantage. Since he used glue and varnish in his woodworking, an open flame was verboten. Obtaining insurance would have been impossible. On the other hand, electric heat was a dry heat, for which he blamed the splitting of his thinnest lumber.

Mr Godyke, it turned out, besides being a cat fancier, was a builder of canoes. That dismal October afternoon, when he saw me standing outside his door in the rain, runny-nosed and bedraggled, he not only didn't laugh or chase me away, he showed concern. "Puss," he said, in a throaty, mellifluous voice that matched his bushy beard and ample belly, "what, pray tell, are we celebrating? This is no kind of day to be outdoors. You should be home by the fire."

We stood there, appraising each other, making eye contact, he through horn-rimmed glasses perched on the end of his nose, I through misty drizzle. He was wearing a blacksmith's leather apron, a colourful plaid shirt and canvas boots. On his head he sported a Greek fisherman's cap, or the remains of one, well sprinkled with sawdust. A pencil, a chisel and a screwdriver stuck out of his shirt pocket. In his hand he held a mallet. Strangest of all, he was chewing an unlit cigar.

"Well, Puss," he growled, "better come in out of the damp. First time I ever saw it raining cats and dogs."

And so I did. I stepped over the threshold and entered a paradise of warmth, light, and best of all, cedar. There were fragrant cedar shavings on the workshop floor, strips of cedar drying in the rafters, blocks of cedar piled helter-skelter. Best of all, there was a lovely cedar canoe under construction in the middle of the shop, missing only its seats. Glancing around, I also noticed a number of paddles and pairs of snowshoes. And in another corner, an oblong box with high sides and a hinged lid.

Though I didn't realize it at the time, I learned later that this box was a sweet-smelling coffin, made of yellow pine. Its presence puzzled me. Especially as Mr Godyke worked at it only spasmodically, and seemingly only when he was in a sombre mood. He took great pains with it, and said he intended to give it at least six coats of shellac. I assumed it was a very special order.

As happened so many times during my journey, Mr Godyke started off by telling me his name. "Friends call me Theo," he said. "Enemies and the missus call me Theodore." Next, he said that I reminded him of a cat he used to own, called Custer. Trouble was, the missus didn't care for cats, and Custer knew this, and went out of his way to be difficult. Scratched the wife's chair. Barfed up fur balls on her side of the bed. Climbed dresses on her side of the closet. Caused tension by standing up for Theo when he and the missus had verbal exchanges and threw dishes at each other. I didn't ask what finally became of Custer. Sometimes it's best not to know.

Theo seemed to sense, even if I didn't, that I'd be there for an extended stay. As I explored the four shadowy corners of his shop, he gathered up a pile of gunny sacks and made me a comfortable nest under his workbench, close to the electric heater. Then he crossed the yard to his house and came back with a bowl of Fancy Feast tuna. "You'll never believe this, Puss," he said, "but I've saved Custer's last tin of cat food, the supper he never ate, as a sort of reminder of him. Or in case I defied the missus and got another cat. Old Custer would be happy knowing it's been put to good use. He hated wet weather too."

So there I was, in out of the damp and cold, nourished, content. Good luck continued to smile on me, though I'm not sure why. The Fates, thank God, were favourably disposed toward me. Guinevere's live-in philosopher, obnoxious Aristotle, after guzzling a litre of Priorato, used to berate those three harmless witches, Clotho, Lachesis and Atropos (dear to the heart of myth-loving Guinevere), whose job is to spin, stretch and sever the thread of life. Short-sighted Aristotle called them vindictive harpies. For an educated man, he was not only a skirt-chaser, he was a dunce.

I resided in Mr Godyke's canoe shed until January, and might have stayed longer, taking refuge from the bitter cold, had not he and his wife set off for their annual sojourn in Florida. During my residency, the weather was consistently atrocious, with wind, sleet and snow.

Through November and December, the temperature never once rose above freezing. And so I was glad to be safe indoors. Nights were lonely, but during the day I had Theo's company. I enjoyed watching him work. He sang and whistled as he formed his cedar strips and tacked them into place. It was fascinating to see a canoe take shape under his skilful hands. Some afternoons, prior to chewing his final cigar, he'd work on the pine coffin. One day, perhaps sensing my curiosity as I crouched at the end of his workbench, he said to me, "Puss, you're probably wondering who this casket is for. Well, wonder no longer. It's for me. When my time comes, I don't want to be planted in no ugly container. So I'm building my own. I've told the missus not to buy me a store-bought mummy case. I've prepaid the funeral, informed the undertaker. No muss, no fuss. Just lower me gently, so's I don't wake up. You'll notice it's lined with the finest velvet. Cost me a bloody fortune."

Speaking of Mr Godyke's wife, in all the time I spent in his workshop, I never once saw her. I still don't know what she looks like. It was as though the canoe shed was off limits to her. She may have been ordered not to trespass. Had she taken a notion to pay a surprise visit, say to ask Theo to drive her to the dentist or the grocery store, she couldn't have, because he kept the door locked. Nor, during the day, did he himself leave very often, except to fetch me a tin of cat food and a bottle of Evian water. He was dedicated to his work. Sometimes he talked on his cellphone, and sometimes, when his canoe-building was not going well, he would step outside for a moment and put a match to the cigar he normally only chewed. On these occasions, I would poke my nose outside too, sniff the chilly air, and thank my lucky stars I wasn't homeless.

I'll say one thing—Theo Godyke appeared to enjoy my company. There were times when he seemed to think of me as his apprentice. He would explain what he was doing, as he bent the ribs of a canoe or screwed the seats in place. He would step aside so that I could see what a good job he'd done. "Perfection, Puss. Utter perfection, if I do say so myself."

With the sweet smell of cedar in my nostrils, I shared his enthusiasm and showed my approval by arching my back and purring when he patted me.

When he wasn't singing to himself, or muttering curses at his disobedient tools, Theo talked about his days in prison. Yes, he'd done time at the Kingston Penitentiary. I never did find out why, but that's where he'd learned canoe- and snowshoe-making. He'd signed up for courses, thinking to kill time, and had found the work enjoyable. Not only that, his instructor, a man named Holloway, had told him he possessed natural aptitude. He amused me by exaggerating the horrors of prison life. By claiming to have been chained in a dank dungeon, subjected to daily floggings, living on scummy broth and maggoty bread. His cell, he used to say, was infested with roaches, which were kept in check only by rats. Speaking of which, he'd managed to tame a fearless brown rat named Vanessa, who would eat from his fingers and sit beside him, washing her whiskers. Had it not been for Vanessa, he said, he might have gone stir-crazy. During his incarceration, he'd made only one bosom friend, a Cuban safecracker named Bolivar, who had a glass eye, spoke English with a Spanish accent, and refused to admit that the invasion of the Bay of Pigs by Cuban exiles in 1961 had failed. Besides politics and safe-cracking, Bolivar dabbled in astrology. Like crazy Minnie from Antigonish, he believed the stars controlled his destiny. He tried to convince Theo that being a Capricorn with Pisces in the ascendancy, and having Jupiter at five degrees for the next twelve months, was tantamount to a death sentence. But all Theo did, besides laugh and shake his head, was tell Bolivar he thought he'd flipped his lid.

Speaking of rodents, in late November, a mouse in the canoe shed caused Theo to briefly lose patience with me and threaten eviction. How was I to know he considered this intrusive creature a pet? How was I to know it reminded him of Vanessa? Until I saw it one morning, sitting at the far end of the workbench, I'd thought that mice hibernated. Evidently not. This one sat there, bold as brass, beady eyes shining, looking delectable. I thought to myself, "A mouse in a canoe shed can't be a good thing. I'll get rid of it for Mr Godyke and have a snack in the process. Maybe he'll be impressed."

It wasn't much of a challenge. Of course, I realize now that the mouse felt safe and secure. She'd let her guard down. She had Mr Godyke to protect her. And so when his back was turned, I snuck up behind her and pounced, as you might sneak up on a nice ripe peach. As I bit into this unfortunate mouse, it gave a panic-stricken squeak of protest, then fell silent. I must admit, it tasted good. As toothsome as chokecherry tarts, my late mother used to say. And so I was momentarily stunned when Mr Godyke threw aside his mallet and shouted, "Hey, that's Myrtle, my tame mouse!"

I could tell he was chagrined, by his tone of voice. I thought he'd be pleased, but he wasn't. He uttered a string of curses, put his fingers in his ears. As a precaution, I jumped down off the workbench and sauntered over behind the coffin, where I stayed till Theo had regained his composure.

It wasn't until he came back from lunch that he called me out of my hiding place and said, "It's not your fault, good buddy. It's instinct. It's probably what Custer would have done. But I was fond of that little mouse. She was a miniature Vanessa. Next time, Puss, show some restraint."

If I'm to be absolutely truthful about Theo Godyke and the several weeks I spent with him, I can't leave out his visitors. They weren't large in number, only a handful, but they were all female and as regular as clockwork. Sometimes they came in the morning, before it was light, sometimes at dusk, but most often after dark. They knocked at the workshop door—three taps, a pause, then three more—and Theo would lay down his tools and let them in. He would help them off with their coats and overshoes, embrace them warmly, and after a brief exchange of greetings, which seldom lasted more than a minute, would lead them to the open coffin in the corner. I won't describe what took place in that narrow box, because I usually averted my eyes. It's not that I'm prudish. I just think some activities should be done in private. Rather than watch, I'd put the time to good use by bathing. I often wondered what Theo would have done if his wife had come knocking, or called him on his cellphone. I wondered if she had any idea what was transpiring behind the locked door of his workshop, where canoes weren't her husband's only hobby.

I don't mean to suggest that every rendezvous took place in the velvet-padded coffin, or that all these women disrobed. There was one, skinny as a scarecrow, with tangled hair and bulbous eyes, who did nothing but stand in the middle of the floor, ankle-deep in shavings, and sing verse after verse of songs I'd never heard. I don't know who she was, or why she came, but Theo always seemed relieved when she left. No sooner would the door have closed behind her than he would go back to work, furiously bending ribs or slapping on varnish, muttering to himself, spitting cigar juice on the floor.

As furtively as they arrived, these nocturnal visitors would depart, usually after much hugging and kissing, and Theo would unwrap a fresh cigar and sit beside his unfinished coffin, thinking his own thoughts. And when, around midnight, he would tuck me into my nest of gunny sacks and go home to his wife, I would smell the lingering perfume of his most recent guest. Often, on his way out, he would say to me, "Puss, it's a good thing cats like you and Custer know how to keep secrets. Otherwise I'd be headed for divorce court, and that could get expensive." He used to call me his watchdog. "Keep an eye on things, good buddy," he'd say. "I'm leaving you in charge. With you as night watchman, I know my canoes will be safe."

Another first for me, while living in Mr Godyke's shop, was sleepwalking. On several occasions, after snuggling down for the night in my nest of gunny sacks, I would wake up next morning in the aromatic pine coffin, with no recollection of how I got there.

A few days before Christmas, Theo went outdoors with a ladder and tacked a string of coloured lights to the eaves. Then he came back in, well frosted, and decorated the coffin with cedar boughs and tinsel. Finally he made space for me on the windowsill, so that I could look out and see festive lights on other people's houses.

Christmas Eve dawned cold and windy. Theo puttered about for an hour, gave the coffin a coat of shellac, then quit work early. In the afternoon he brought me a slice of pâté and a dish of cream, and said he felt badly about leaving me alone, but his wife had invited her mother and widowed aunt over for eggnog and his presence was required.

I tried not to feel lonely, but couldn't help remembering other Christmases, when Guinevere had given me catnip toys wrapped in tissue paper and encouraged me to rip them open. Aristotle, her scowling Scrooge, disapproved of the way I pulled baubles off the tree and made a general mess. He would have locked me in a closet if he'd had his way. I wondered where he and Guinevere were spending Christmas this year. Probably neither of them alone, like I was, with no one to talk to, or even scold me. I'll admit feeling sorry for myself. Who wouldn't? As darkness fell, I heard the wind whistling under the eaves, sighing at the door. Through the window I saw the sky full of stars. I wished Theo were there. Or Hattie and the Sandsuckers. Which sounds like a musical group. Or those estranged sisters, Minnie and Muriel. Or Queenie. Or Priapus. Or Mr Plimsoll. Or best of all, my lovable Guinevere.

But I was alone in a canoe shed full of scented shavings. I didn't know when Theo would return. He'd said he might have to go visiting with the missus. Might have to sample his sister-in-law's fruitcake and sing carols around her piano. Hopefully, there'd be rum in the eggnog, but he doubted it. Usually she served glasses of abominable sherry, such as Harvey's Bristol Cream, or some other repulsive, sissified beverage.

Thinking these mournful thoughts, I climbed into the velvet-lined coffin and settled myself for what the poet calls "a long winter's nap." Since I was already inside the coffin, I had little fear of sleepwalking. Drifting off, I could have sworn I heard Guinevere whisper, "Merry Christmas, Rufus."

*

SIX
Green-Eyed Angela and the Trafalgar of Neebing Marsh

On New Year's Day, before handing me my eviction notice, Theo explained why it was necessary. He and his wife were taking the bus to Fort Lauderdale. They'd be gone two months, maybe three, living in a rented room under the palms, two blocks from the ocean. Mrs Godyke's arthritis and disposition would benefit enormously. Warm, sunny days, mild nights. Idle hours on the sand, watching bathers and windsurfers. Foolhardy youngsters skimming the waves under billowing kites. Seafood for supper. Theo, gregarious by nature, would stroll the beach, white as a beluga, belly hanging over his trunks, talking to tourists from Idaho. Obviously, they couldn't take me with them. But not to worry. Theo knew a young couple, related in some way to his singing night-time visitor, who lived on the top floor of a house on Ray Boulevard. Their names were Lester and Magdalena. They were quiet, sensible folk, expecting a baby in April, and most important, they liked cats. As a matter of fact, before moving to Ray Boulevard, their prize possession, a calico kitten named Pinky, had set them at odds with their previous landlord, a hateful tyrant named Mahoney. Ironically, no sooner had they given Mahoney notice and signed a lease for their new lodgings, than Pinky had come down with feline nephritis and expired. And so getting another cat, if it were healthy and independent, and didn't mind being alone all day while they were at work, would suit them perfectly.

Fine, but I hated the thought of leaving Theo's workshop, with its sweet-smelling cedar canoes and mysterious pine coffin. I knew I'd miss Theo too, his conversation, the tapping of his little hammer. One thing I wouldn't miss would be the annoying nighttime visitations. Another would be the stench of varnish. Those irritants I could live without.

On the afternoon of my departure, as Lester and Magdalena placed me in a cat carrier and prepared to take me away in their minivan, Theo said a strange thing to me. He said, "Now, listen, Puss, you've been great company, I've enjoyed having you, but all good things must come to and end. I'm sure you'll be happy with Lester and Magdalena, but if for any reason you aren't, or they aren't, I'll take you back when I return from Florida. What I don't want is to get an e-mail saying you've gone AWOL. Not at this time of year. You'd freeze to death. And don't get the notion you can live in the canoe shed by yourself. You can't. It's impossible. The door will be locked, the heat turned off. So be a good cat and go with Lester and Magdalena. Enjoy their hospitality. Be there for the blessed event in April, when you'll become an uncle."

And that was it. Theo was gone. By then, like Minnie from Antigonish, I should have been used to being abandoned. Huddled in my carrier, not liking the car ride one bit, I said to myself, "It could be worse, Rufus. At least you'll have a home, and someone to look after you." Still, as we approached Ray Boulevard in the minivan, I had a lump in my throat the size of a crab cake.

What can I tell you? In the time I spent with them, Lester and Magdalena treated me well. They gave me a varied menu, bottled water, a high-tech electronic litter box. They combed and brushed me, bought me toys, clipped my nails. On cold nights, they let me sleep at the foot of their bed. My only complaint was that I was never allowed outdoors. At first, I missed the smells of the street, the feel of dirt under my paws. I missed being able to sniff bushes where other cats had left olfactory messages. But since the city was buried to the eyeballs in snow, which the north wind sculpted into tall drifts, and since Lester and Magdalena were away all day, except on weekends, when they shopped and went to church, being housebound was probably a good thing.

Lester taught history at Hillcrest High School. Magdalena was a dental hygienist in Dr Jayapurra's clinic on Clavet Street. Her hobby was needlepoint, which she did while seated in a rocking chair, watching television. Lester spent all his spare time working on a historical novel which he hoped to publish. Every evening, and much of Saturday and Sunday, surrounded by reference books, he toiled at his word processor. I sat on the windowsill beside him, looking out at the snow-clogged boulevard. Apparently forgetting I was a cat, not a person, he would talk to me as he wrote, testing dialogue, asking my opinion as to the believability of his story. As nearly as I could tell, it described a bloody conflict between the conjoined cities of Fort William and Port Arthur, prior to their amalgamation in 1970. It started with a political skirmish on Memorial Avenue, where Port Arthur's welcome arch used to be. Proponents of the name "Lakehead" for the new city hurled invective at those who favoured "Thunder Bay." Respective police forces were summoned to quell the disturbance. Threats were made, challenges accepted. Cooler heads did not prevail. Brickbats were tossed, bystanders beaned. At dusk, the two militias were called out. But instead of settling things and dispersing the crowd, soldiers took up opposing positions and the donnybrook was on. Reinforcements were sent for. Both mayors appeared and were handed megaphones. But instead of pleading for calm and stopping the disturbance, they began calling each other names. As night fell, bonfires were lit. Boards were torn off outbuildings for fuel. Floodlights were brought in by both contingents, with the idea of blinding the enemy, but sharpshooters soon put these out of commission. The Lake Superior Regiment answered a call to arms on the Port Arthur side with a still-functioning Bren gun carrier, to which the Fort William Armoury responded with a battery of obsolete two-inch mortars. Meanwhile, sailors from HMCS *Griffin* steamed south in their leaky bumboat, thinking to surprise the Fort William flotilla, but were themselves surprised by a flag-bedecked, ceremonial cutter which charged out from behind McKellar

Island, bow cannon aimed, but not firing due to a lack of ammunition. Her captain said later that he would have arrived in a moth-balled Corvette, except that no one knew how to start her engines. This absurd naval engagement was referred to in the *Daily Times Journal* as "The Trafalgar of Neebing Marsh."

At times, Lester would leap from his chair and wave his arms theatrically, re-enacting battle scenes in his mind. Such animation might have been amusing, had it not been frightening. His shouts would bring Magdalena running to see what was the matter. Lester would say things like, "Under a smoke screen, the scurvy Fort Williamites have just sent an unmanned streetcar, loaded with greased pigs, into the Port Arthur barricades!"

"Yes, dear," Magdalena would say, and return to her needlepoint, while I took refuge under the bed.

During the dark days of January, when I wasn't sleeping, I spent a lot of time gazing out the kitchen window. Occasionally I saw other cats, fence-walking or sitting on their back porches, and wished I could go down and join them. Maybe strike up a conversation, exchange life histories. There was one cat in particular, a white part-Persian with green eyes, who struck my fancy. I think she liked me too. She lived four houses away, and on sunny afternoons was permitted outdoors on a leash. She seemed to enjoy lunging at birds, but could never catch one, because of her restricted movement. She was tied to her porch railing, and the birds, knowing this, teased her. Had I not felt sorry for her, I might have laughed. One day, lashing her tail in annoyance, she looked up and saw me at my window.

She studied me, seemed interested, but what could either of us do? I was housebound, she was tethered. We were destined never to meet. Not unless one of us escaped, and that seemed unlikely. Ours could only be a silent, long-distance relationship. There was an attraction between us, and that's what made it frustrating. Who knows how compatible we might have been? Involuntary confinement can be cruel.

On Valentine's Day, Lester gave Magdalena a dozen roses, while she gave him a harmonica. The flowers I could understand, but not the mouth organ. I think Magdalena came to regret her choice. No matter how hard Lester practised, he never succeeded in making music. The sounds he produced were discordant at best. Not that he didn't try, but his enthusiasm did not begin to make up for his lack of talent. To shut out his tuneless wheezing, Magdalena took to wearing headphones, plugged into a Sony Walkman. I had no such defence. When it got too much for me, I crawled into the furthest depths of the hall closet and buried my head in galoshes. By the end of the month, Lester knew as well as anyone that he was wasting his time, and we all breathed a sigh of relief when he put away the harmonica and returned to his historical novel.

Looking back, I think what intrigued me most about Lester and Magdalena was their suppertime conversation. After not seeing each other all day, they had things to talk about. They began talking the moment they came in the door, pausing only to take off their coats, pour cocktails, and put frozen dinners in the microwave. I found it quite pleasant, as the kitchen filled with cooking odours and my dish of Fancy Feast was replenished. Darkness would have fallen by the time we sat down to eat. The evening news, usually horrific, would be on television, but irrelevant. Lester would recount the antics of his students, which were no different than the antics of his colleagues at staff meetings. Magdalena would name the youngsters who had bitten Dr Jayapurra's fingers, and the mothers who had propositioned him. Once those mundane topics were out of the way, it would be time for gossip and dessert. That's how I first learned that another cat would be coming to stay with us for a week. A halitosis specialist named Reginald, who also worked in Dr Jayapurra's clinic, had been called out of town, and his cat, Angela, needed temporary shelter. When Lester asked where Reginald was going, Magdalena explained that he'd been summoned to an institution down east, in which his severely handicapped son was a patient. The boy's name was Ennis, and he'd been born with physical defects so severe that there was little hope of caring for him at home. At least that's what Reginald and the doctors thought. Reginald's wife, however, disagreed. She refused to let Ennis be institutionalized. Over Reginald's protests, the boy was entrusted to her and she looked after him for the first eight months of his life. But then she herself suddenly fell ill and died. And so Ennis had ended up back in Toronto, where, despite his late mother's misgivings, he was given the best of care and attention. Two or three times a year, Reginald visited him, monitored his progress, offered advice as to treatment. And now, at the end of February, it was time for just such a visit. Previously, Reginald had put Angela in a kennel, but since Magdalena lived nearby and already had a stray cat showing signs of loneliness, it was decided that Angela would come and stay here. To which I had no serious objection. I was, after all, a non-paying guest myself.

Imagine my surprise when, a few mornings after the above conversation, who should arrive at the door in Reginald's arms, wearing a stylish flea collar and accompanied by her own toys and litter box, but the white, part-Persian beauty I'd been admiring from my lofty window. Introductions were hardly necessary. When Angela was presented to me, I totally lost my suavity and blurted, "Well, Angela, your name certainly suits you."

Brilliant. She smiled but didn't laugh, for which I thanked her. Lester said, "How about that? You'd almost think they knew each other."

And so while Lester and Magdalena were away at work, and Reginald was in Toronto, Angela and I spent a congenial week together in my garret on Ray Boulevard. We ate up all the special treats provided, got high on green Colombian catnip, quenched our thirst with Evian water. We spent hours talking and looking out the window. We shared life's disappointments and unfulfilled dreams. We also shared nightmares. Angela said she had a recurring one, in which she was infested with crawling bugs, worse than mites or chiggers. Another involved a loutish, romantically inclined tom, who had one thing on his mind, and one thing only. By the end of the dream, he'd have transformed himself into a ham-handed vet.

We sat side by side on the back of the couch, took long naps in the sun, groomed each other's whiskers. We were so compatible and at ease that you might have mistaken us for an old married couple. I must say, I was captivated by Angela's looks and personality. In morning light, her eyes were jade green. Late in the day, they turned turquoise. She was really quite lovely, and I told her so. I don't think she'd heard it often enough. Not that her good looks were accidental. She spent a large part of every day before the mirror, primping, ensuring that every hair was in place, every eyebrow just so. When I jokingly referred to my own toilet as a lick and a promise, she said I was typical of most men. I said that in my young, unaltered days I might have asked her to run away with me, hit the road, go travelling. She said that in her young, unaltered days, she might have accepted. Not now, though. Not and give up all these hard-won creature comforts. Not unless a dashing young millionaire came along, with promises of luxury condos, satin sheets and winters in Hawaii.

At the risk of boring her, I told her the story of my odyssey thus far. She listened politely, until I came to Theo Godyke's velvet-lined coffin, and then showed a little more interest. What she preferred, though, was watching *Animal Planet* on TV. Her favourite program was "Dogs with Jobs." Every evening after supper, when Lester and Magdalena fell asleep on the couch, Angela would laugh herself silly watching dogs do dumb things for the camera. I'm not sure why she found these canine antics amusing, but she did. Which was fine with me. I enjoyed watching her as much as I enjoyed watching them. Maybe more. I remember the night they showed Labrador retrievers jumping into an icy bog after rubber ducks. They looked so eager to please, so anxious to be appreciated. "Look at them," Angela scoffed. "What idiots. Can you imagine a cat behaving like that? Doing someone's bidding just because it was expected. And for what? A pat on the head? A soup bone? You wouldn't catch me chasing ducks in a heated pool, never mind in a beaver pond. I'd say, 'Go retrieve your own damn duck, Davy Crockett. You shot it, you fetch it!'"

Of course the day of Angela's departure came all too soon. Reginald returned from Toronto in a sombre mood and took her home with him. I barely had time to say goodbye. Not until she'd left did I realize I hadn't asked her about Reginald's ex-wife and invalid son. I'd meant to. Her views might have been insightful.

 The apartment seemed empty without her. Empty, yet confining. Days dragged. Time lay heavy on my paws. I became bored, disgruntled. I took out my frustrations by scratching the furniture and climbing halfway up the drapes. When Lester, more tolerant of my moods than Magdalena, tried to console me, I hissed at him. Magdalena's advancing pregnancy was putting us all on edge. One night I heard her ask Lester if he thought having a cat and a newborn infant in the house was a good idea. Next day a postcard arrived from Theo in Florida, saying that he and his wife were staying away an extra month.

 And so one March morning, after a sleepless night of looking out the window and feeling sorry for myself, I came to the conclusion that I must soon be on my way. Not that Lester and Magdalena hadn't been good hosts. But days were lengthening, snow was melting, icicles were forming along the eaves. Crows were congregating in the poplars. Grosbeaks perched on telephone wires. These were early signs of spring. I could feel my wanderlust returning. I was on a mission, after all. An interrupted mission, but a mission nonetheless. I couldn't wait for Theo to come home, any more than I could wait for Magdalena's baby. Like Odysseus in lotus land, I sensed a danger in overstaying my welcome.

One sunny afternoon, a few days after these reflections, Lester and Magdalena's landlord came upstairs, bearing a boxed crib. As he let himself into the apartment, I made my exit. I crept down two flights of stairs, squeezed out the front door, and for the first time in a long time felt fresh air on my face. I must say, the smells were delicious. I detected damp earth, cat spray, mouldy leaves. My nostrils were assailed. My brain reeled. I stretched, shook myself, took several deep breaths. The spring sun felt good on my fur. Bare patches of earth showed through the melting snow. I could hear birds chirping, sewers gurgling. Winter's grip was loosening. I felt like cheering.

I'm not sure why, but I directed my steps along the sidewalk toward Angela's house. I may have planned to say goodbye to her. I may have planned to ask her if she'd like to accompany me. Or perhaps all I wanted was to hear her wish me luck. Imagine my surprise, therefore, when I discovered a grotesque bulldog chained in her back yard, barking like a hellhound. Screaming children were playing tag. A red-headed woman in rubber boots, smoking a cigarette, supervised them. It looked like a freak show. Like hallucinations from uncut Venezuelan catnip. I ducked out of sight before any of them saw me. For a moment, I wondered if I'd approached the wrong house. But I hadn't. This was Angela's house all right. Or at least it had been. Now it was obviously being used as an asylum.

And so I turned my back on Ray Boulevard, pointed my nose south toward McKibbin Street, and closed the book on yet another chapter of my peripatetic adventure. As I stretched my limbs and called on muscles I hadn't used lately, I remember having two thoughts. First, that I was glad to see winter in retreat. And second, even though Angela had obviously moved away, I was happy to have known her. I suppose that's what memories are made of.

*

SEVEN
A Night with Alexi at St Elmo's Church, Another in the Coach House of St Joseph's Manor

It was to be a day, then a week, of unexpected detours. That first mild afternoon, I noticed a funeral cortège travelling slowly west on Beresford Street. As I'd never been to a funeral, I fell in behind the last mourners and followed them along Hodge Street as far as St Elmo's Anglican Church. At first, I thought the procession might be part of an Easter pageant, such as they have in the Spanish provinces of Catalonia and Andalusia. But it wasn't. It was the real thing. I learned this from a grizzled old Russian blue named Alexi, the caretaker's cat, who lived in the church basement. Alexi was sitting beside the hearse, getting some sun on his arthritic limbs, when he saw me crossing the parking lot. He said he hoped I wasn't planning to attend the burial, which would entail a twenty-minute car ride to the cemetery. He said, "Sorry, boy. No provision for family pets."

I walked over to him, sat beside him on the grass. "I'm not a family pet. I don't even know the deceased."

He looked surprised. "You don't? You're a transient?"

"I'm on my way to Lake Street. I've just come from Ray Boulevard."

He didn't seem overly impressed. I wondered if he might be a bit hard of hearing. Senior cats often are. Overhead, church bells chimed. Inside, I could hear an organ playing. Alexi rose, stretched his hind legs, gave me a sceptical look. "If you don't know the deceased, what are you doing here? I hope you're not morbidly curious."

"I'm curious," I said. "But not morbidly. And you?"

He went in through a side door, started down a shadowy stairway. Since he hadn't told me not to, I followed him. "I knew her slightly," he said. "A nice old lady from the neighbourhood. Sundays, she brought me fish-flavoured kibble wrapped in a napkin. Which I ate, to please her. I can't stand dry cat food."

At the far end of the basement, where the floor was tiled, chairs and tables had been set up. Bands of sunlight streaming in through ground-level windows gave the place an ecclesiastical look. In a dim little kitchen off to one side, grey-haired ladies in aprons were making sandwiches and setting out plates of shortbread. "For the reception later," Alexi explained, as though I couldn't see that for myself.

He obviously knew his way around. He walked right up to the kitchen door and sat there, meowing, until one of the ladies tossed him a morsel of ham. As infirm as he was, or pretended to be, he caught the ham in mid-air, snaring it with an extended forepaw, as you would a butterfly.

"I see you've brought a friend," the lady said, throwing me a morsel of ham too. Unprepared, I missed it, but pounced quickly, fearing that if I didn't, Alexi would. As I chewed, he gave me a disdainful look. The ham was filling, but a bit salty for my taste, so when the sandwich-maker threw another piece, I let Alexi have it. Then we stepped aside, as two ladies carried out a large coffee urn and plugged it in. "For the reception later," Alexi said. "Third time this month. I may have to go on a diet."

"So this is what funerals are all about? Eating sandwiches, drinking coffee?"

Alexi snorted. "Hardly. The main event is upstairs. Folks come to pay their last respects to the person in the coffin."

"I know all about coffins. The last place I was at, a gentleman was building one for himself."

Alexi frowned, gave me a look of disbelief. "No kidding?"

"No kidding. Out of yellow pine. Lined with velvet."

As I followed him into the caretaker's room, which was full of mops and floor polishers, Alexi said, "The woman in the coffin upstairs spent her last days in a nursing home. I hear they treated her badly. She couldn't recognize her own husband, her own children. It was like she had no family. Hardly even knew her own name. She stopped coming to church when they put her in the nursing home. I hear they cut off her hair, took away her shoes. She used to bring me dry kibble in a napkin. But when she couldn't find her way to and from church, they stuck her in a facility. Tell me, Leo, what's wrong with people? Now she's dead. Nice old lady. Never hurt anybody. Could you manage another sandwich? It may be a while till the next one."

"I'll pass, thanks, but you go ahead."

"Lunch meat gives me heartburn. Maybe it's the mustard. It's getting so I associate funerals with heartburn. But I ask you, what's wrong with people?"

"It's the way of the world, I'm afraid."

"The way of a sick world, Leo."

"My name's not Leo. It's Rufus."

"I call any strange cat Leo. What would you prefer? *Simba*?"

"My name is Rufus."

"Rufus? That's a terrible name. You should think seriously about changing it to Leo."

Upstairs, the organ had stopped. Bells pealed. We could hear a shuffling of feet, and then out in the parking lot, car engines starting. "They'll be on their way to the cemetery now," Alexi surmised. "When they come back, they'll be hungry. They'll come down here and have sandwiches. I once rode to the graveyard in a hearse. I went for a ride in a police car too. I've never ridden in an ambulance or fire engine, but someday I will. My friend the caretaker has connections at City Hall. Where he goes, I go. As soon as those ladies turn their backs, let's you and me see if there's any tuna. Last funeral, they had tuna. How's your sniffer? Mine's pretty well shot. It used to be good, but now it's in decline, like the rest of my organs."

"My sniffer's fine," I said. "But I really should be on my way. I still have to find a place to spend the night."

Alexi's mouth fell open. "Spend the night? Are you crazy, boy? You'll spend the night here. My caretaker and I have all the comforts of home. There'll be leftover cookies. There always are. Table scraps. Cheese and pickles. Lemonade. We'll have a feast. Tell stories. My caretaker will read the newspaper aloud, like he does every evening. Did I tell you he used to be a public school janitor, but got dismissed for some trumped-up perversity. So you can't leave now, Leo. Not before the wake."

To be truthful, I didn't like the sound of this. The thought of being read to by the caretaker did not entice me, nor did the prospect of being surrounded by hungry mourners. So I'm not sure why I stayed. Perhaps out of curiosity. Perhaps because it was too late in the day to set off. Nights were still cool, the streets not bare by any means. I hoped I wasn't going soft, which is the long-distance traveller's downfall.

In any event, I stayed. I spent the night with Alexi and his caretaker. At this remove, I have no regrets, other than the stomach ache that resulted from too many bits of gristly ham, passed to us under the tables by octogenarians. They munched the shortbreads quite well, and drank their beverages, but the gristle in the lunch meat defeated them. Where Alexi and I sat, at shin-level, it was raining (in Alexi's words) processed pig. We gorged ourselves, tried to outdo each other, as is the nature of competitive cats in the wild.

There was something almost Kafkaesque about the scene in the basement of St Elmo's Church that day. The babble of voices, the laughter, the clinking of cups and saucers. I don't know where the caretaker was during all this, but Alexi and I were under the tables, receiving tidbits from cat-loving parishioners. I felt bewildered, as though I'd metamorphosed into a floor-crawling bug. As though I'd strayed into an unorthodox society, whose customs I didn't understand. Of course, Alexi didn't share this view. To him, because he'd seen it all before, this was normal. It made sense. As the brouhaha approached a crescendo, I half expected the old folks to get up and start dancing. Red-faced serving ladies in aprons, hair askew, bustled out of the kitchen with fresh trays of goodies.

Eventually, when the mounds of sandwiches and cookies had been reduced to crumbs and the first rush of caffeine had worn off, the room became quiet. People stopped talking. A few shed tears. I suppose this was the calm after the storm. A time for solemn introspection. A few old-timers actually nodded off, while others were still chewing. Some held hands. Some brushed crumbs off each other's faces. Even at a wake, appearances were important.

"Alexi," I said, "does any of this seems strange to you?"

He belched, gave himself a lethargic scratch under the chin. "Not to me, boy. I'd say it's pretty much run-of-the-mill."

If there was a signal, I missed it, but just then, an orderly exodus began. Chairs were pushed back, people began leaving. The ladies in aprons gathered up dirty dishes and took them back to the kitchen. A few final scraps were tossed our way. I was reminded of a TV documentary at Lester and Magdalena's apartment, which showed tame monkeys being hand-fed at a Sri Lankan monastery.

My diary of accomplishments will show that I spent a night of gastric distress in the basement of St Elmo's Church. Not many cats can make that claim, or would want to. When things had quieted down, when the last mourner had left, Alexi and I repaired to the custodial chambers for a postprandial nap. He curled up on the caretaker's cot, while I built a nest on a stack of cleaning rags. The caretaker made his appearance soon after—an elderly gentleman with white whiskers and horn-rimmed spectacles, wearing running shoes, a béret and a tan smock. His nose dripped. I could not quite imagine him committing perversity in a public school. His name, according to Alexi, was Mr Puttgarden, and sure enough, just when I was dozing off, he started reading aloud from the *Chronicle-Journal*. Which made it difficult to sleep. His reading was interspersed with chest-rattling coughs and exclamations of displeasure at stories he didn't like. After an hour or so of this, in the midst of the obituaries, I crawled underneath my pile of rags and immersed myself in polyester. Until I moved, I don't think Mr Puttgarden had noticed me. I heard him ask Alexi who I was, but by then Alexi was comatose. If he answered, I didn't hear him. Mr Puttgarden, keeper of the catacombs, harrumphed and went on with his reading.

I left at first light, thirsty from all the ham, cheese and shortbread, but fairly well rested. Alexi was still dead to the world. During the night, he must have been dreaming, because long after Mr Puttgarden had stopped reading aloud, I heard Alexi moaning and groaning in his sleep. He might have been suffering his usual heartburn. I heard him cry out, "Who let that three-headed dog in here?" Speaking of Mr Puttgarden, he was already raking gravel in the parking lot. Though it was a mild, sunny morning, with the promise of blue skies and calm winds, he had his hat and coat on, and a scarf around his neck. When he saw me he expressed surprise that I wasn't staying for the wedding that afternoon. "Alexi will be sorry he missed you. He doesn't get many visitors these days. As a matter of fact, neither do I. If it wasn't for weddings and funerals, we'd only see people on Sunday. Folks ain't as spiritual as they used to be. Bad sign, if you ask me. Too much religion on TV. Folks don't take it serious no more. Come back when you can stay longer."

I left him leaning on his rake, coughing, wiping his nose. As for me, I had a choice to make. I could head either south toward Cornwall Avenue or north toward Red River Road. Without much hesitation, I chose Red River Road. At the outset of my journey, Queenie's friend Priapus had said he thought I should stop in at St Joseph's Heritage, just off Carrie Street, where the good Sisters of Saint Joseph could be counted on to give succour to a wandering cat. He'd said that his friend Hildegarde was a frequent guest at the old stone manor house, which the nuns used as their residence.

With the manor as my destination, I lost no time. I hightailed it across Red River Road during a lull in traffic and hurried down the back lane behind Martha Street. Though I'd never been to St Joseph's Heritage before, its tall white buildings were easy to spot. I homed in on what I assumed must be the manor house, an imposing stone mansion from an earlier age, off from the rest of the complex, surrounded by stately firs. I remember thinking to myself that this would be an ideal locale for cats as well as for nuns. There was a secure, peaceful air about the place, with its vine-covered coach house, its porticos and casement windows. It had a brooding, Edwardian air about it, yet did not look spooky or haunted. I pictured it as the vacation home of a duke. I also imagined it full of cats, living contentedly on its several levels with grounds to prowl, trees to climb, a rock wall to sit on. I imagined nuns escorting geriatric patients about the grounds in summer, stopping to pick flowers and feed the squirrels. There were stone benches on which to rest, and cool, shady bowers, where you could turn your back on the world, read a book, think peaceful thoughts. I was glad to be viewing it on a mild spring day, with pigeons on the roof, rather than in dark December, when it might be mistaken for a Russian winter palace on the Siberian steppes.

You can imagine my crushing disappointment, therefore, when I encountered not an enclave of glossy, well-fed cats, as I'd anticipated, but a solitary, bedraggled, nondescript brown Manx. He was skulking about the back door, meowing forlornly. When he saw me, he stopped meowing, gave me a fierce, unfriendly look. In a voice that was almost a squawk, he said, "Who the hell are you and what do you want?"

After being so warmly welcomed the day before at St Elmo's Church, I was ill prepared for such belligerence. "If it's any of your business, my name is Rufus and I'd been hoping for some charity. Last fall I was told I might find hospitality here with the Sisters of St Joseph."

The scrawny Manx took a step toward me. I didn't know whether he intended this as a threatening gesture, or simply had bad eyesight. "Well, you won't find it here."

"Won't find what here?"

"Charity. Hospitality. Whatever the hell you just said. You won't find any nuns, either. They've moved. Nowadays, this here's an Alzheimer's hospice. People inside need more help than you do, whistle-pig."

"I don't believe you."

"Doesn't matter whether you believe me or not. It's the truth. There's no nuns here. Trust me. I heard they moved to Old Fort William."

"I was told they'd be here."

"Well, they're not. Whoever told you that was either stupid or misinformed. There's a lot of that going around these days. It's an epidemic."

I had the feeling the Manx was enjoying my frustration and disappointment. I also didn't like his tone. It was on the tip of my tongue to say that a cat with no tail was like a ship without a rudder. But I didn't. I said, "So, if that's the case, what are you doing here?"

The Manx shook his head, flicked his tail. "I live nearby. I come over to hunt. There's mice in them old flower beds. You ever catch mice, whistle-pig?"

"Of course I catch mice. I'm quite good at it. But why do you call me whistle-pig? Why would you call anybody that? My name is Rufus."

"Well, Rufus, you don't look like a hunter. You ain't nearly mean or skinny enough. You look more like a whistle-pig, which is what I call interlopers. I hope you're not planning on staying. There ain't mice enough for us both, and I was here first. So if I was you, I'd push on. Before I call in reinforcements and clobber you."

What posturing, I thought. How wearisome. How fake. "What reinforcements? Didn't you say you were alone?"

"Well, not entirely alone. I got friends. How about you, whistle-pig? You got friends?"

"My friend Priapus said he knew a cat here named Hildegarde. He said I should ask for her."

"There's no Hildegarde here. If there ever was, she's long gone. Maybe she went to Old Fort William with the nuns. Ain't nobody here but me and the forget-me-nots. I have myself for company, and that's the way I like it."

"It appears to me you also have a large chip on your shoulder. What's your name?"

"Scum Bag, but you can call me Scum for short. And that's not a chip on my shoulder. That's attitude. I'm a cat with attitude. These days, you need attitude to survive."

"Oh, please. Spare me. Next you'll be telling me what a hard life you've had. How nobody understands you. How you live by your wits. I've heard it all before."

"So, you think you're tough?"

"For a whistle-pig, I'm tough enough. I've walked here from Skyline Avenue, which is more than you can say. I don't mope around an old convent, feeling sorry for myself. And I'm on my way to Lake Street, so you don't have to worry about me invading your territory."

"Hey, you think you can take me? You feel like going a few rounds? I have priority here, that's all I'm saying."

"You also have a load of insecurities. Yes, I think I can take you. I'll go a few rounds, if that's what you want. No holds barred, and if I win, the manor house is mine."

This was all bluff on my part, but in my travels, and especially during stopovers, I'd developed a sixth sense about bravado. Something told me that Scum Bag the Manx was not nearly as brave as he let on. Besides, what did I have to lose? All roads led south, and from here on, south was downhill.

Sure enough, Scum Bag backed up a few steps. His fierce grimace was cracking. With his broken whiskers and bald spots, not to mention his missing tail, he was on the verge of comic relief. I almost felt sorry for him. He was, after all, only defending his turf. Or what he thought was his turf. He wasn't a cat with attitude, he was a cat with self-doubt. Angela would have laughed at him. I pictured him running from the really tough cats I'd seen on Rockwood Avenue, the day I arrived at Mr Godyke's canoe shed. I arched my back ever so slightly, flattened my ears, showed a bit of tooth.

"Whoa, now, whistle-pig," Scum said, striving for sarcasm, but visibly impressed. "Let's not get carried away here. Let's be civilized. I hardly even know you. Maybe there's room for negotiation."

"Yes," I said. "Let's negotiate. For starters, you can stop calling me whistle-pig. My name is Rufus. I suspect you're known by something other than Scum Bag."

He let out his breath, seemed to relax. "My real name, if you must know, is Frederico, but nobody ever calls me that. Like I told you, they call me Scum, which I don't mind, so long as it's said in jest."

As tensions eased and conflict seemed averted, we folded our paws under us and crouched on the damp flagstones, directly under a fire escape. From inside the manor, we could hear people's voices and bursts of joyless laughter. Looking up at the building's opaque windows and sombre façade, I realized I'd lost all desire to enter. Especially since the Sisters of St Joseph now lived elsewhere.

    I'd also pretty much lost interest in Frederico. I did pay attention, though, when he said that before coming to the Heritage he'd lived in a commune of cats under Saskatchewan Pool Elevator Six, down on the waterfront. Until it was demolished with explosives a few years ago, it had been the only home he'd ever known. The reigning potentate was a tolerant, enlightened Burmese known as the Marchesa, who, along with her palace guard, presided over underground tunnels and kept the young safe from predators. Mice were plentiful, because of the silos full of grain, and incoming rail cars were always accompanied by flavourful pigeons. In summer, one's diet was supplemented with minnows and crayfish, which were fun to catch.

    "They blew it up with no warning," Frederico said. "No alarm bell. No loudspeaker announcement. We figured something was up, watching them plant their charges around the footings. Many cats lost their lives the day of the explosion. Not to mention pigeons and seagulls. They say it rained corpses for a good five minutes. Raining cats and dogs, except there weren't no dogs. I would have lost my life too, had I not been away on a twenty-four-hour pass, visiting friends on Court Street. When we heard the explosion, we rushed outdoors, but all we saw was dust settling. And people cheering the removal of an ugly eyesore from the waterfront. I have to tell you, it took a long time to get over the trauma. I still have flashbacks. Would you believe it, half my fur fell out. My tail looked like a rat's. I had no eyebrows, no whiskers. Quite different from the feline victims buried in the rubble, whose claws kept growing for weeks after they died. Landscapers coming across them couldn't believe the length of their claws. It's not the first time I'd heard of that. Apparently human corpses behave the same way, except with them it's hair and fingernails."

I didn't know what to say, so said nothing, which Frederico took as a signal to keep talking. "As bad off as I was, I still came out better than my friend Hector, a Maine Coon from Current River, who was one of the Marchesa's palace guards. The day of the explosion, he was out on an errand, and the elevator blew up just as he arrived home. He wasn't killed, or even injured, but the blast knocked him senseless, and while he lay there unconscious, a flock of starlings came and pecked out his eyes. Can you imagine? When he woke up, he was blind as a bat. Me and my Court Street friends found him sitting there, surrounded by starlings and crows, and after we chased away the vultures, we did what we could for Hector. Which wasn't much. He kept asking what had happened. We didn't rightly know ourselves, but we knew it wasn't good. We left matronly Florence with him, because she'd once lived with the nurses at the Port Arthur General. Next day, one of the bulldozer operators, who liked cats and felt sorry for Hector, picked him up and took him home. Last I heard, he was living over on Pine Street, making the best of his infirmity. If you're going by that way, you should look him up. He's on the corner of Pine and

Van Norman. Despite being sightless, he's a very personable cat, as most Maine Coons are. And he likes hearing what visitors have to say. Since he can't see, that's how he gets his news. Tell him I said hello."

I remembered that historic explosion. I was living with Guinevere at the time, in her Bayview apartment on Lake Street, and I recall hearing her say, "Rufus, I do believe they've blown up old Saskatchewan Pool 6, either accidentally, or on purpose."

I assured Frederico that if I happened to be going by the corner of Pine and Van Norman, I'd stop in and see Hector.

He said, "Some of us hurried down there afterward, and it was a sorry sight. Nothing but rubble and shattered concrete. Dead bodies all over the place. No survivors. Not even the Marchesa, who'd had a premonition the night before. She'd told everyone to leave, but few did. They didn't take her seriously. She was always having premonitions. What a mess. And so quiet. All you heard was crows cawing as they flew down for body parts. Later, there was songbirds, who sang louder than usual, because the concussion had deafened them. I lost my brother and sister, both parents, aunts and uncles. I went and lived under a chicken house on Tupper Street for a while, then in an attic on Machar Avenue, and finally here. But it hasn't been easy, whistle-pig. I mean Rufus. It hasn't been easy at all. In fact, it's been damn hard. So if I have hangups, it's understandable, don't you agree?"

If he expected sympathy from me, he was due for disappointment. Not that I didn't feel for him, but he struck me as someone who expects you to listen, then doesn't reciprocate. In this world, there are talkers and listeners, and he was a talker. He would not have been interested in the account of my journey. Still, I was curious, and so I asked him what life had been like under the elevator. Before he could answer, the back door of the manor opened and a thin old lady in a green shawl placed a brimming dish of assorted table scraps on the ground, right under our noses. She said not a word, made no attempt to pat either of us, and was back inside with the door closed before we had a chance to thank her. So this was what Frederico had been waiting for. This was why he'd wanted me to leave. Emitting a low growl, he buried his face in the food and began hauling out chunks of corned beef. Though there was more than he could possibly eat, enough for five cats, he obviously would have preferred not to share. But since I was hungry, and not intimidated by his ugly manners, I began gobbling too. I also emitted what might have been construed as a growl. The dinner was tasty, especially the gravy, and in a short time all that remained was a bit of cabbage. Frederico demonstrated his appreciation with a tremendous belch and sat back on his haunches.

I said, "Do you always eat this well, Frederico?"

He thought a moment, unwilling to admit he did, in case I recognized a good thing and stayed. On the other hand, he was anxious to impress. "Not always," he said, washing his forepaws and whiskers. "Sometimes they forget all about me. Sometimes they put the food out early and it's all gone by the time I get here. And sometimes they put pepper on everything, which ruins it. When the nuns were here, they never used pepper. But you were asking about life under the elevator. To be honest, the place was full of freaks and outlaws. Every day there was fights and violence. Love triangles. Love rectangles. Hexagons. The Marchesa and her palace guard did their best to keep the lid on, but sometimes they couldn't, especially when saxifrage was in bloom or someone found a maggoty trout washed up on shore. Idiots rolled in the carcass and came home high as kites, stinking of fish. Some cats aren't happy unless they're causing trouble. You know the type. Can't leave well enough alone. I remember once there was an uproar when a Havana Brown named Oliver tried to usurp the Marchesa. The palace guard came in and expelled him by force. I heard he tried to organize rebels on the outside, but nothing ever came of it. So maybe the demolition was a good thing. It got rid of some bad apples. It got rid of everyone else too. These are troubled times we live in, whistle-pig. By the way, I never met your friend Priapus, but I remember Hildegarde. She got along well with the nuns. She was their favourite. I think they might have taken her to Old Fort William, or wherever they went. She was allowed indoors during cold weather. In summer she used to hang out on the fire escape, or in the coach house, right there behind you. She had it fixed up nice. I'm surprised no one has moved in. It's obvious she's not coming back."

I left him licking gravy off the boiled cabbage and went over to explore the coach house. It had seen better days. At one time it must have provided shelter to the nuns as they climbed in and out of horse-drawn buggies and sleighs. Now its stone walls were crumbling and its roof needed patching. Only one of its windows still had glass in it. But I could see where

Hildegarde must have had her pad, in an alcove on the far wall, which at one time might have been a closet for harnesses. There was still some loose hay, and the remains of a horse blanket, and because of its homey feel, I crawled in and made myself comfortable. As darkness deepened, I was quite snug, in out of the wind, safe from prying eyes. I could hear Frederico muttering to himself, saying he wouldn't sleep in a disused coach house unless he was paid to. I hoped he'd go away and leave me in peace. I was tired of the sound of his voice. "Frederico," I called out, "what time is breakfast?"

"Are you planning to spend the night there?"

"I am. In Hildegarde's old bed. I feel very secure. What time is breakfast?"

"Well, it varies. Sometimes seven, sometimes eight. You may have to fend off the crows. And cats from Martha Street."

"See you at breakfast, Frederico."

He must have taken the hint, because I heard nothing more from him. In Hildegarde's horse-blanket nest I was warm, weary, full of corned beef stew. Some music would have been nice, and someone reading me the newspaper, but when you're on a solo pilgrimage, you have to make do with what you have.

Breakfast was served not at seven or eight, but at six-thirty. I was awake, listening to robins, when I heard the manor door open. So I got up and wandered over, and saw Frederico with his face buried in cornmeal mush. There were several other cats with him, lined up, waiting their turn. They looked askance when I strode to the front of the line and shouldered Frederico aside. "I can see why they call you Scum Bag," I said to him. "If I'd listened to you, I'd have missed breakfast altogether."

With the edge off my hunger, I returned to the coach house for a quick clean-up, took my bearings, and planned my itinerary. It showed promise of being a nice March day, with sunshine and gentle winds. I almost convinced myself I could detect distant harbour smells. It was a month early for the first ship of the season, but Frederico's talk of grain elevators had made me anxious to see the waterfront.

*

EIGHT
Hector, Martha and Bertha, Giuseppe's Gold Mercedes

That morning, heading south, I stuck pretty well to Van Norman Street. Just as I crossed Madeline, a block west of Pine, the sun burst out from behind low clouds and I could feel its warmth on my fur. I must say, it felt good. I detoured briefly toward Tupper Street to avoid dogs, then regained Van Norman. I was happy to be walking, happy to be free of Frederico.

I wasn't really looking for blind Hector when I saw him. From Frederico's description, I wasn't even sure I'd recognize a Maine Coon. But there, guarding the front steps of the first house on Pine Street, basking in the spring sun, was a brown, long-haired cat with a bushy raccoon tail and blank eye sockets. I knew it must be Hector. So I crossed the road for a closer look. One thing I noticed immediately was the way Hector's ears were in constant motion. He might not be able to see, but his hearing was obviously keen. I hadn't made a sound, yet I suspected he knew I was there. His nose was pointed right at me as he followed my progress. As I sat down at the far end of his driveway, I saw him lift his head and stick out his tongue, as though tasting the air. He didn't answer, at least not right away, when I said to him, "Is your name by any chance Hector?"

Finally he said, "I can't seem to place your voice, mate. Do I know you?"

"My name is Rufus. You don't know me. I'm on my way from Skyline Avenue to Lake Street. I've been on the road all winter. I spent last night in the coach house at St Joseph's manor. Your friend Frederico suggested I stop and say hello."

Hector twitched his ears, flared his nostrils. "Skyline Avenue to Lake Street? That's quite a hike. And in winter. You must be a bear for punishment. By the way, mate, if it's the same Frederico that used to live under Sask Pool 6, he's not exactly a friend. We hung out together for a couple of years down at the elevator, but since the demolition and my loss of eyesight, I haven't seen much of him. I'm sure he has better things to do. When I could have used his assistance, the day the grackles got me, he took off with his friends. We used to call him Scum Bag."

This differed slightly from what I'd heard. "Frederico told me they went looking for survivors and left you with a nurse."

"With a nurse? She was no nurse, mate. She was a clueless old tart named Florence who told me my blindness would be temporary. Two or three days at the most. Hah!"

"I believe Frederico said they were starlings."

"Well, they weren't starlings, mate. They were grackles. That's what the tractor driver who found me said. Not that it matters. Starlings, grackles, who cares? They pecked out my eyes. Up till then, I thought only crows did that. Why don't you come set a spell? Tell me about your trek. I'd be interested to know why a cat would undertake such an ordeal. Not that it hasn't been done before, but *in winter?*"

It turned into an interesting morning. Hector told me that before he lost his vision, he himself had once walked all the way from Sask Pool 6 to Boulevard Lake, just to visit a gorgeous silver tabby named Hilda. It took him two weeks, and wasn't worth it, because by the time he got there, Hilda had fallen for a Peke-faced Persian. He also told me that contrary to what most folks thought, his ancestors hadn't come from Maine, but from France. He said that during the French Revolution, Marie Antoinette, on the eve of her execution, had sent a dozen of her favourite cats to America aboard a ship bound for Tadoussac. For some unknown reason, landfall was made at Portland instead, where the cats were unloaded and given homes among the local gentry. Ever since 1793, people have thought that bushy brown regal cats with raccoon tails and ruffs around their necks came from Maine, when actually they came from Versailles.

While he was telling me this, people went in and out of his house—adults, children, even a scruffy, foul-smelling poodle. They all said hello to Hector, bent down and patted him, let him smell their fingers. The poodle stuck a wet nose in his ear, gave him a lick across the chops, which made Hector grimace and shake his head, but you could tell he appreciated the attention. All this time, his ears twitched like antennae and his whiskers fairly bristled. During a lull in the traffic, he said to me, "Correct me if I'm wrong, but I get the impression you're a young, muscular cat, heavy through the shoulders, with a plumed tail and pale green eyes."

"Very accurate," I said. "All except for the eyes. They're hazel, or so I've been told. And I'm not all that muscular, or as young as you might think."

Just then the door opened and a girl of six or seven placed a bowl of chicken-flavoured Tender Vittles on the floor between us. "I hope you can stay for lunch," Hector said, after the girl had gone back inside. "I don't get many visitors since my mishap. It's funny how folks tend to forget you once you're incapacitated. All I can say is, thank God for bulldozer operators and their families. Would you believe it, mate, until I got used to the house and knew where everything was, they followed me around and made sure I didn't fall down stairs. They nursed me back to health and only laughed at me when I bumped into things. I mean, why did they bother? What use was I to anyone? They fed me, bathed me, steered me from room to room. You'd never know it, but there was a time, before my other senses compensated, when I thought the family dog was a small person with bad breath."

As we munched our Tender Vittles, he told me about life under the elevator, before demolition. He said that the great love of his life after Hilda had been a spotted tabby named Lilith. "She was well named, mate. Of course, you know who Lilith was."

"No, can't say that I do."

"In Semitic folklore, Lilith was Adam's first wife. She was dispossessed by Eve. Mainly, she haunted lonely, deserted places. My Lilith was beautiful, mate. Spotted tabbies usually are. But arrogant and stand-offish. I had to work hard at keeping her affection. It was worth it, but a struggle. I brought her treats. She had a taste for curlews and brown moles that were hard to catch. She was addicted to wild mint. I defended her in arguments with the Marchesa, which caused friction. Her namesake, Lilith of the Semites, had a nasty habit of killing newborn babies, about which I'll say no more."

He said that under the elevator he'd had two close friends—a sorrel Somali named Juba and a Cornish Rex named Eddy. Neither cat had been in residence on demolition day, thank goodness, but afterward, of course, they'd had to find new lodgings. Juba meandered over to the District Jail on North Algoma, where he befriended guards and inmates alike and was soon made mascot. Eddy, the Cornish Rex, had found a home over at the Psychiatric Hospital, also on North Algoma, where they offered him the position of honorary night watchman. It was nice, Hector said, to see old friends go out into the world and become useful. Unlike that slouch, Frederico, who talked a good fight but seemed to feel no social obligation. The name Scum Bag suited him.

I asked Hector if being blind had changed his outlook on life. He said he thought that being deaf might almost be worse. "It's bizarre, mate, but in my dreams, I see perfectly, and in living colour. I see cats, dogs, old cronies from the elevator. I see parrots with fluorescent plumage, peacocks, rainbows, lions, tigers, red-headed girls. Once, I even saw an elephant. I also see visions during the day. Premonitory visions. Car crashes, ladies fainting, pots falling off stoves. Trouble is, I can't communicate. I can't warn people. It's frustrating as hell. I've also developed telepathic powers. Even without seeing their faces, I know what cats, dogs and people are thinking. Which is not always good, mate."

I might have stayed longer, might have spent the entire afternoon on Hector's doorstep, had not the same seven-year-old girl come out, picked him up and carried him inside. I heard her tell him it was time for his nap. He meowed in protest, but not very loudly, and I had the feeling he wasn't all that perturbed. You could tell he wasn't used to having long conversations. I also suspect he may have felt a bit sorry for himself, knowing I could see the real world, could travel in it, while all he had were memories and hallucinations. Had he been able, he might very well have traded his comfortable security for a sighted adventure. Who knows? In any case, he was gone, and since I wasn't invited in, I took my leave.

It was a fine day to be outdoors, walking through a quiet residential neighbourhood. There were no parrots or peacocks, but as I trudged along Elizabeth Street, on my way to Red River Road, I heard, and then saw, my first robin. With a belly full of Tender Vittles, I suppressed the urge to chase her. She was standing in the middle of someone's front yard, one eye on me, the other on the ground, as though hoping to see a worm. "Bird," I said, "I have things to do, places to go. And I've just eaten. Otherwise we'd do lunch. My main concern is getting safely across Red River Road. If you'd care to meet me on the other side, we could talk."

At that, the robin gave me her undivided attention. She seemed prepared for flight. At the corner of High Street, I looked back, and though she was still watching me intently, she now had a long earthworm dangling from her beak. It was with a measure of disbelief, tinged with admiration, that I saw her tilt her head back, stretch out her neck, and swallow the worm. Not all at once, but with a series of bobbing jerks. I found it an amusing, though not particularly appetizing spectacle.

I crossed Red River Road at the busy High Street intersection, darting from a juniper hedge on one side to a yard full of hollyhocks on the other. I timed my crossing so as to take advantage of an unhurried funeral procession, possibly on its way from Sargent's mortuary to St Elmo's Church. Most passing vehicles stopped, or at least slowed down, but some didn't. One that didn't was a yellow school bus. Unfortunately, I was counting on it to give way to the hearse, and so I had to scamper the last few metres, or be run over. As if this indignity weren't enough, the bus driver, a florid-faced woman smoking a cigarette and wearing a baseball cap, honked her horn at me. I responded with the only weapon in my arsenal—a dismissive flick of the tail. If she'd possessed a fraction of Hector's telepathy, she might have jumped off her bus and chased me. As it was, I cleared a white picket fence and a stone wall in a single bound and scurried under the hollyhocks for protection.

Looking around, I saw I was in a spacious yard full of birch trees, at the centre of which stood a red brick Victorian mansion. All the houses on north High Street are sumptuous—the homes of doctors, lawyers, business tycoons. This particular one was surrounded by flower beds and gravel pathways. As I snuck out from under my hollyhock bush, intending to press on down High Street, I looked across the street and saw a gold Mercedes pull up behind Hillcrest Towers. A man wearing a blue suit got out, left his window rolled down, and went into the apartment building. Nothing unusual about that, but what amazed me, moments later, was the emergence from the car of two large lilac Persians. By the way they were both yawning, I suspected they'd been asleep. Stretching and scratching, they jumped down and began sniffing tires. I assumed the man in the blue suit would soon come and take them indoors, if that's where they lived, and roll up his car window. That's what I assumed, but that's not what happened.

I'll admit I've had limited experience with cars. Generally speaking, I dislike any conveyance with four wheels and an engine. I try to avoid them. I don't like riding in them, and I certainly don't like having to dodge them in traffic. So it puzzled me to see these two stunning mauve cats treating the Mercedes as though they owned it. Exactly what messages they were decoding by sniffing its tires, I couldn't even imagine.

It was while they were thus occupied, and I was perched on the garden wall across the street, that they both glanced up and saw me. I wouldn't say they looked surprised, only curious. Next thing I knew, they came bouncing across the pavement, hurdled the white picket fence, and leapt gracefully up beside me. With swishing tails and Cheshire smiles, they introduced themselves.

Their names were Martha and Bertha. They were twin sisters, descended from prize-winning Persian parents, and yes, they lived in Hillcrest Towers, in a third-floor apartment, with the owner of the gold Mercedes, whose name was Giuseppe. Exactly what Giuseppe did for a living, they weren't sure. It might have had something to with surveillance cameras or adult videos. The important thing was, he provided for his cats. In nice weather, he allowed them to spend lazy afternoons on his balcony, from which vantage point they could keep an eye on the neighbourhood. Summer nights, they liked to watch lavish garden parties, complete with Chinese lanterns and wandering musicians, which were held in the front yard of the red brick Victorian mansion.

They said that Giuseppe loved and appreciated cats. He fed Martha and Bertha Swedish fish balls, gave them bottled water, took them on frequent car rides. Morning and evening, when they were let outdoors to prowl the grounds of Hillcrest Towers, he left a window in the Mercedes open for them, in case they needed a safe refuge from dogs or boys. Countless times, they'd had to jump into the car to escape a neighbour's ill-mannered Doberman. Street kids, fearful of ruthless Giuseppe, knew better than to mess with his gold car or its contents. Seems he had a reputation for being vengeful. He also had power over people, and while Martha and Bertha didn't quite understand this, neither did they question it. The only person Giuseppe didn't have control over was Mr Kunkel, the concierge of Hillcrest Towers, who steadfastly refused to install a cat door in his building. He feared the place would be overrun with strays. Giuseppe called him a callous ingrate, after helping him hook up a surveillance camera in his bedroom, with the idea of catching his wife entertaining ex-boyfriends. Kunkel had long suspected her of infidelity and wanted evidence to confirm his suspicions. The irony was that Giuseppe himself was guilty of visiting Mrs Kunkel. And so, after installing the video camera, he invited Mrs Kunkel to his apartment instead.

Martha and Bertha said that on these occasions, they got a real eyeful, but didn't make a fuss, for fear that Giuseppe would banish them to the balcony.

I must say, it was very pleasant, there on the garden wall, surrounded by hollyhocks and stately birch trees, in the company of Martha and Bertha. They said they'd just come back from a memorial service in South Gillies. At first I thought they meant they'd been in the funeral procession that had blocked my crossing of Red River Road. But they said no, Giuseppe had driven them to a farm on Highway 595, where they'd paid their last respects to an elderly female cat named Miss Kitty. It was a sad event, they said, because Miss Kitty, rescued fourteen years ago as a half-frozen stray and cared for by a noted rural journalist, had been a boon companion. Though recently infirm due to old age, Miss Kitty would be fondly remembered and sadly missed. Giuseppe, a close friend of the journalist's family, had choked up during the eulogy.

On the way home from South Gillies, they'd stopped at a rustic tea house in Murillo, where Giuseppe knew everyone and where cats were welcome. Later, while they were detained at a railway crossing east of town, awaiting the passage of a freight train, a dozen black-capped chickadees, caught in the slipstream, had tumbled from the sky and crashed on the roof of the Mercedes. Bertha said the patter of their bodies sounded like large hailstones. Of course, the sisters had hoped Giuseppe would get out and gather up the warm corpses for a feast, but he didn't. Or rather couldn't, because by then a dozen automobiles were lined up, impatient to proceed. So Martha and Bertha, instead of feasting, had curled up in the back seat of the Mercedes and fallen asleep. Which explained why they were yawning and stretching when I first saw them.

"Birds falling from the sky isn't all that unusual," Bertha said. "One cold winter's night, just as we stepped out on our balcony for a breath of fresh air, a family of nuthatches came rolling down off the roof and landed at our feet. They were numbed by carbon monoxide, from sitting too close to the chimney. We ate as many as we could before they woke up. Next day we regurgitated feathers all over the apartment. Giuseppe vowed to disown us if we ever did it again."

We might have spent longer in the Victorian mansion's garden, swapping stories and getting acquainted, had not Giuseppe himself appeared on his balcony across the street. When he spotted Martha and Bertha he put two fingers in his mouth and gave one of the shrillest whistles I've ever heard. A delivery van going by slammed on its brakes. So did a city bus. Pigeons took flight. Crows in the birch trees began cawing. It was an unearthly, camel-driver's whistle, such as you might hear at night in the Gobi desert.

"That means we must leave you, babe," Bertha said. "Giuseppe wants us home. He's probably going out in the car."

Martha concurred. She stood up, stretched, shook a forepaw. "To make a video, no doubt. He's always making videos. Sometimes he films himself in the apartment with buxom women. We're in quite a few episodes. If you look closely, you'll see us. We're not the stars, not like Mrs Kunkel and Giuseppe, but we're there. Once we sat in front of the camera and they had to reshoot the whole scene. Mrs Kunkel didn't mind, but Giuseppe wasn't happy. He put us out on the balcony and shut the door."

"Listen, Rufus," Martha said, wiggling her shapely rear end as she prepared to jump the picket fence and head for the street, "if you're ever back this way, stop in and see us. Maybe we'll have a cat door by then. We'll invite you up for dinner. Maybe watch a video."

Bertha was already at the sidewalk, waiting for the light to change. "Babe," she called out, "if you continue down High Street, you'll come to our cousin Alfie's house. Chances are, he'll be out on his front steps, sunning himself. You can't miss him. He's a mottled tortie-tabby with a face like a broken shoe. He pretends to be tough, but he has a strong feminine side. He's a marshmallow, an artiste. You'll like him. Tell him we sent you."

And then they were gone. I watched the two of them gallop across High Street, tails held high, like frisky ponies. In the afternoon sun, their lilac fur fairly glistened. I was sorry to see them go, but when Giuseppe whistled, you didn't stand around waiting to see what he wanted. Not if you hoped to go riding in his gold Mercedes.

If Alfie, the mottled tortie-tabby with a face like a broken shoe, was sunning himself that afternoon, I didn't see him. Maybe he was indoors, looking out a window, keeping an eye peeled for the first ship in the harbour. As I trudged by, it occurred to me that invisible Alfie was a lucky cat, living in such a fine big house, with such a spectacular panorama spread before him. In the foreground, Hillcrest Park, with its manicured lawns and symmetrical flower beds. In the middle ground, further down the hill, the city's Finnish and Italian sections. And beyond that, the rail yards, elevators and waterfront, my eventual destination. On a clear day, from an upstairs window, lucky Alfie would see the Welcome Islands and the legendary Sleeping Giant, guarding the harbour entrance.

Weighted by these envious thoughts, I started down the Dufferin Street hill. As I did so, I noticed clouds moving in from the west. A cold, sleety drizzle began to fall. Winter wasn't giving up without a fight. As I approached the ochre sandstone façade of Barnabas Safe Haven & Family Centre, I wondered what my chances were of seeing a flock of chickadees fall off the roof and plunge to earth. Probably close to zero. Then I perceived lights on inside, and a sign above the door: "Everyone Welcome." Did that include cats? We would soon find out. Thinking of Miss Kitty, recently gone to meet her maker, I turned my steps toward those lighted, beckoning windows.

*

NINE
Stopover at Barnabas Safe Haven with Ursula and Hermione

It snowed that night. Not much, only a centimetre or two, but still, it was good to find shelter from the damp wind and sleety drizzle blowing in off the lake. "Everyone Welcome," engraved in stone above the front door of Barnabas Safe Haven & Family Centre, halfway down Dufferin Hill, didn't exactly refer to cats. I don't mean that cats weren't welcome. They were, so long as they went around to the back, where there was a closed porch full of shelves and sacking. A number of cats were already in residence—homeless waifs, I assumed, substance abusers, unwed mothers. As I entered, shaking droplets off my fur, I could see eyes watching me from the gloom. I counted a dozen or so noses sticking out of makeshift nests and hammocks, mostly up near the ceiling, where it was warmer. There seemed to be a bit of grumbling at my presence, but no overt hostility. I mean, no one said, "Oh, brother, look what the cat dragged in." It struck me as the kind of place where you might find refugees from elevator demolitions, cats in transit, cats on hiatus, cats waiting for balmy weather. Listening, I thought I detected mumbled greetings, but wasn't sure, because of the variety of accents. Which was not surprising, considering that below Dufferin Hill there's a veritable hodgepodge of ethnicity. Barnabas Safe Haven is, after all, only a stone's throw from the Finlandia Club, the Scandinavian Home and the Italian Cultural Centre.

When I thought of Martha and Bertha in their third-floor apartment at Hillcrest Towers, and of Alfie, in his High Street mansion, I was filled with restless envy. I imagined those pampered cats turning up their noses at a flophouse full of unfortunates, such as Barnabas Safe Haven. But here I was, on an inclement March night, with nowhere else to go. Had the weather been better, I might have pressed on. As I was standing there, mulling things over, the back door flew opened, light flooded out, and a major-domo in boots, béret and cassock emptied half a bag of dry cat food on the ground. No plates of table scraps, as at St Joseph's Heritage. No bones. No bottled water. Cats of all stripes and sizes crawled out of their hammocks and began crunching. While they were doing this, the same steward (if that's who he was) went round the enclosure, sprinkling flea powder on all the bedding. He dusted every sack, every nest, making sure, as he did so, that the occupants were all away eating. When he came to me, he said, "New in town, Tovarich? Here's a pad for you, if you want it, right beside Hermione, who babbles too much, never shuts up, could talk the hind leg off a horse, but means well. Try to overlook her annoying giggle. She's a bit high-strung. There's them that can't stand her. Don't be bashful about dinner. Only one sitting. You miss it, you go hungry. So don't stand on ceremony. Dig in, like everybody else. This ravenous pack of freeloaders won't leave a crumb. They call me Mahatma, by the way."

Hermione, the giggling cat, was a lumpy blonde Balinese with olive, slightly crossed eyes. I noticed that after eating only a few mouthfuls of kibble, she turned her attention to the well-gnawed root of a dwarf cedar growing alongside the porch. "Don't mind me, Amigo," she giggled, when she saw me watching her. "I spend my winters at the Conservatory, where I've developed vegetarian tendencies. I don't know what I'll do if I go back to sea when navigation opens. I doubt they'll have cedar root aboard my tugboat. So I'm chewing on this while I still can. If I could, I'd begin a herbal diet. Sardine-flavoured nuggets don't do it for me any more. Taste like mouldy slippers. Ham bone I don't mind. The tugboat I was on last summer, *Point Valour*, had a cook who believed ships' cats should eat nothing but meat. Everything from pemmican to jugged hare. She called us carnivores. Trouble was, eating so much flesh killed our incentive for catching rats. My shipmate, a Turkish Van with one yellow eye and one blue, who fancied himself a stud and spent his free time looking in mirrors, lost his job because of rats. Couldn't be bothered catching them. The captain put him ashore one day at Keefer Terminal, told him there was a beefcake contest, sailed away without him. We were just as happy. All he ever talked about was the prizes he'd won as a show cat. I doubt he was ever in a show. Thought he was the cat's pyjamas, if you know what I mean. Where are you from, by the way? You look vaguely familiar. Ever been a ship's cat?"

Tucking into the Iams, which was chicken-flavoured, not sardine, and tasty as well as filling, I assured Hermione I'd never sailed, nor had any wish to. I told her I knew all about cedar root, ginger root, dogwood root, balsam root, and all the other aromatic roots, which, like betel nut, give you an addictive buzz but not much nourishment. Not that I have anything against addictive buzzes, but at the moment I was just plain hungry.

Hermione giggled. Her eyes were already slightly glazed. "You don't look to me like you've missed many meals, Amigo. Not like these other scarecrows who've spent the winter living out of garbage cans."

"Nor do you," I said.

"Touché, Amigo. But I'll have you know I was once considered glamorous. Before I hit the streets, I had my picture in the newspaper, reclining on silk cushions. I lived with a socially prominent family on High Street. Until the lady of the house got pregnant, and was told by some quack witch doctor that having a cat around could cause embryonic brain damage. So they got rid of me. Put me in a shelter called Hollyland Haven, from which I escaped, con spirito. Imagine their surprise when I showed up at home one day, somewhat a mess, but wiser and reasonably intact. So they took me out Onion Lake Road in a wicker basket and turned me loose. This time I got the message and headed for Marina Park. I'd always had a thing about boats."

"Did you say Hollyland Haven?"

"What if I did?"

"I once knew a cat named Hortense who spent time at Hollyland Haven. They called her Hattie for short."

"Well, I never knew no Hattie or Hortense. Cats with names like that should stay incognito. There was a pot-bellied pig though. I don't think he had a name. Or if he did, I forget it."

"How about a Burmese named Quigley?"

"Never heard of him. But then, I didn't socialize much. Those Hollyland cats were so common, Amigo. I can't begin to tell you. Not a thinker among them. On High Street there were at least some brains, some intellectuals."

"I don't suppose you ever ran into Martha and Bertha, twin lilac Persians?"

"To tell you the truth, Amigo, I avoid Persians of any colour. Too full of themselves, too uppity. I knew a tortie-tabby named Alfie, though. Lived in a château across from Hillcrest Park. Swaggered up and down High Street like Billy the Kid. Nice disposition, with a prizefighter's face. Said he was a lady-killer and prodigious mouser. I never saw evidence of either."

"Maybe in his younger day."

"Maybe. So what brings you to Barnabas Safe Haven on a sleety March evening? Can't be lust for adventure. Love affair gone wrong? Down on your luck? Off to join the French Foreign Legion? In need of a friend?"

I sensed from her giggles she wasn't really interested in why I was there. I started to say, "Well, it's a long story, Hermione. I'm on my way to Lake Street . . . "

But that's as far as I got. "Lake Street?" she said with a giggle. "The engineer on my tugboat was from Lake Street. Or was it Front Street? I think it might have been Front Street. His name was Higgenbottom and he took a shine to me. Let me sleep in a box beside the engine. Fed me rare roast beef. Whenever we escorted a Salty, he kept tabs on me, because cooks on some foreign vessels consider stewed cat a delicacy. Oriental sailors clamour for it. More than once, Higgenbottom saved my hide, when sneaky deck hands slid down ropes and tried to shanghai me. Sometimes they offered him money. Five dollars a kilo, skinned. You hear what I'm saying, Amigo? If it hadn't been for greasy old Higgenbottom, I could have ended up in a casserole with bean sprouts. Now, I'm not prejudiced, and I deplore racial profiling, but I'd rather be here talking to you than in some Chinaman's belly. Shiver me timbers. Helm amidships. Anchors aweigh. Steer me right if I'm wrong. It's a small world. Where did you say you were going?"

"Lake Street."

"Now that you mention it, I believe Higgenbottom lives on Lake Street. He was married once, but his wife left him. Gave him a choice, her or tugboats. So he chose tugboats. Said they were easier to maintain and less noisy. You know what he does in the off-season? He blows glass figurines and writes letters to the editor. He's a complicated man, is old Higgenbottom. Loves engines, can't stand stuffy bureaucracy. Calls himself a social activist, which means glorified shit-disturber. He and Mahatma should get together. Birds of a feather. You don't talk much, Amigo. Cat got your tongue? What if these are the good old days? We keep hoping for something better, but what if it's all downhill from here? You ever think of that? I do. This may be as good as it gets. Enjoy it while you can, is my motto. Tomorrow may be worse."

After supper, as I made myself comfortable in my burlap cubicle and listened to Hermione prattle, I wasn't sure how long I'd stay. Looking out, I saw that the sleet had turned to snow. Flakes the size of goose feathers were falling, sticking to the ground. Overhead, treetops swayed in the wind. From inside Barnabas Safe Haven came the sound of gospel music, as though a prayer meeting were in progress. It had been a long day, and as I composed myself for sleep, lulled by Hermione's chatter and other muffled voices, I decided that unless the weather improved dramatically, I'd be in no rush to leave. Dozing off, I reflected on how lucky I'd been the past few months, finding shelter when I needed it, a square meal now and then, cats to talk to, people who cared. Under a gruff exterior, you often found kindness.

The snoring and muttering of my cellmates kept me awake for a while. Hermione finally stopped talking and began humming Dolly Parton songs. I fell asleep with the sweet melodies of "Just Someone I Used to Know" and "Coat of Many Colours" echoing in my ear. In those unlikely surroundings, halfway down Dufferin Hill, I confess I slept like a baby.

I spent a week at Barnabas Safe Haven—six days longer than I intended. During that time I got to know several of the semi-permanent guests (they preferred not to be called inmates), among whom the most interesting was probably Ursula, an elderly female tortoiseshell with white whiskers and a majestic tail. I'm not sure how long Ursula had been there. She wasn't sure herself. If you asked her, she might say two years, or she might say six months. She sometimes spoke in riddles and non sequiturs. The only thing she was consistent about was where she'd lived previously, which was with two Finnish ladies, mother and daughter, in a clapboard house on Banning Street. She said that the old lady, Anneli, a grey, skeletal woman, never came out of her room. She lay in bed all day, watching television, shouting at Helvi, her daughter, to bring Diet Cokes and doughnuts. That's what she survived on. Diet Cokes and doughnuts. Which seemed to agree with her, because she outlived Helvi and was still going strong when the younger woman keeled over in the kitchen one day and could not be revived. Paramedics were summoned by Anneli, who complained to them that her negligent daughter was three hours late with lunch. It took stern words from the paramedics to convince her that Helvi was lying dead on the kitchen floor, and if she wanted lunch she'd have to get it herself.

Ursula said she wasn't sure what eventually became of Anneli. After Helvi's funeral, the clapboard house on Banning Street was put up for sale. She herself wandered the neighbourhood all summer, living hand to mouth, catching chipmunks and baby robins. In the fall, when nights grew cool and dogs ran in packs, she cast about for a place to stay and stumbled upon Barnabas Safe Haven. Mahatma had invited her in, and she'd never left.

"You should be here in summer, Dufus," she said to me one morning after breakfast, while we were sitting by ourselves in a patch of sunlight, minding our own business. "It's like a miniature jungle. Toucans come flying through, hornbills, bushtits, green budgerigars."

"Excuse me," I said, "but what's a budgerigar?"

"A tropical bird, Dufus. Your common budgie. Comes in assorted colours. Tasty, once you get past the feathers. Mahatma frowns on the poaching of exotic birds. Unfortunately, they tend to screech when caught, so it's hard to do it secretly. Your friend Hermione, whom I can't stand, by the way, dumb blonde blabbermouth, is very adept at snagging jackdaws. She climbs trees after dark and nabs them where they roost. I dislike her methods, but have to give her credit. She's the best jackdaw catcher we have. She once caught a racing pigeon. Should have heard her crow about that. Till Mahatma found out—then she sang a different tune. Blamed it on rat-tailed Beulah, the Siamese, who couldn't catch a chill."

"Ursula," I said, "are you sure all those rare birds you've just mentioned actually fly this far north?"

She gave me a wink and a smile. "Would I pull your leg, Dufus? Believe me, I've seen rarer birds than those. I've seen auks and bluebills. I've seen fulmars and frigate birds. Once, I even saw a cassowary. We're on the main migration route, you know. We're on the great circle flyway."

"I don't think so, Ursula. I think those birds are imaginary."

"What birds?"

"The birds you've just been talking about. By the way, my name is Rufus, not Dufus."

"I thought you said Dufus. I could have sworn you said Dufus. But listen, I wasn't talking about birds. It's a subject that doesn't interest me. I have more important things on my mind. Such as what happens to us when Mahatma retires or gets called up to defend his country against rebels."

"Rebels? What rebels?"

"There's always rebels, Dufus. When they come whooping out of the swamp, thick as alligators, we'd best be ready."

One afternoon we sat and watched the sun melt the last of the newly fallen snow. Rivulets of brown water trickled down Dufferin Hill, making a pleasant splashing over sewer gratings. A young Scottish Fold named Malcolm climbed to the top of a spruce tree and announced the arrival of the first ship of the season. Some cats expressed doubt that he could see the harbour from Barnabas Safe Haven, and even if he could, that he'd know a ship from a shoehorn. "Come down from there!" they shouted at him. "Stop being so silly. Stop spreading false rumours. Who do you think you are, the town crier? The first ship won't be here for another month."

Malcolm came scuttling down the tree backwards, still insisting he'd seen smoke on the horizon, out near the Sleeping Giant. "Why would he say that?" I asked Ursula.

She gave me a sly look. "Because I told him to. We have a pool, as to the arrival of the first ship. Today was my pick. If we could have convinced these ignoramuses, I'd have won. But we didn't. They're smarter than I thought. Last year, it worked perfectly."

Later she remarked that Malcolm reminded her of one of her grandsons, always inventing stories, always clamouring for attention. He'd wake everyone from a sound sleep, warning them that wild dogs were on the loose, causing unnecessary panic.

When I asked her how many grandchildren she had, she said she didn't know. She'd lost count. "Dozens, I suppose. It's not the kind of thing I'm proud of, although some cats would be. Every time I see a swarm of alley cats, or hear how full the shelters are, I'm sorry for my contribution. I'm afraid I showed little restraint. All those one-night stands, back when I was young and foolish. Seemed harmless at the time. Now my own offspring don't recognize me. If I knew where half of them were, I'd be lucky. They won't miss me when I'm gone, 'cause they won't even know. And if they knew, they wouldn't care. Would you believe, my first serious affair was with my cousin Boris? My parents forbade me to have boyfriends, but considered Boris part of the family. Like a brother. Little did they know. When they asked me who I wanted as chaperone, I said Boris. So they appointed him. Some chaperone. He's the one who needed a chaperone. The kittens looked just like him. Our parents put two and two together and excommunicated both of us. But that was a long time ago, Dufus. Now everybody thinks I'm senile. Nothing left to do but fade away. Maybe it's true. Some days I feel the end is very near. I see those garish birds, the ones you say don't exist. Not only see them, but hear them. I may be old, but I still have feelings. I appreciate my next of kin, even if they've disowned me. We should be thankful for our friends too. Are you my friend, Dufus? Or do you think of me as a simpleton? I wish I knew what reality was. I wish someone would put a sock in Hermione's mouth. Are you aware of her infuriating habit of saying good morning to every single person and calling us all by name? She does it to show off, just to prove she can. It's a quirk, a mania.

Every damn morning! If you ignore her, she pesters you till you give in and acknowledge her. She demands that you acknowledge her. She's a cracked old cat."

"Maybe she's just being friendly."

"Maybe she's obsessive-compulsive. It's like when she bathes. She counts the number of licks. Counts out loud. Twenty-two licks on this side, twenty-two licks on that. Never twenty-one or twenty-three. Always exactly twenty-two. She's out of her tree, Dufus. Speaking of which, I wish I could still climb trees. Like Malcolm. Maybe I'd see ships too."

In her lucid moments, when she wasn't fantasizing, Ursula was one of the few people I met during my travels who seemed interested in hearing about Guinevere. She would say to me, "Tell me about Gwendolyn, your mistress. What kind of person was she?"

"Do you mean Guinevere?"

"Yes. Guinevere. Isn't that what I said?"

"You called her Gwendolyn."

"Well, you once told me her name was Gwendolyn. Or Genevieve. Or Gilgamesh. How am I supposed to keep track?"

"Her name is Guinevere. That's all I've ever called her."

"So, tell me about Guinevere. Was she a gentle woman?"

"Yes, very gentle."

"Kind?"

"Very kind."

"Generous? Intelligent?"

"Reasonably."

"Did she have faults?"

"None that I detected."

"Was she conscientious? A good housekeeper?"

"She was adequate. I had no complaints."

"Did she protest when you scratched the furniture? Object to your fur balls?"

"No, but Aristotle, her brainless boyfriend, did."

"Is that why he left?"

"There were other reasons. He was an idiot. I remember the last big argument they had. The one that ended it all. He said to her, 'Just suppose, Guinevere, that God, if there is a God, offered you a choice. You could either be the last person on earth, to whom all the secrets of the universe would be revealed—how big it is, what its boundaries are, when and how it began, when and how it will end, the exact location of Heaven—or, instead, and this is important, so listen carefully, you could discover a cure for cancer tomorrow and share it with all mankind. Which would you choose? Tell me, *which would you choose?*' And Guinevere said, 'I have no idea. Anyway, they're both impossible, so it's a stupid question to begin with.' And Aristotle, the jackass, said, 'You refuse to answer? You refuse to play my game?' And Guinevere said, 'Yes, I do. I refuse to play your stupid game.' And he said, 'If you don't answer, I'm leaving. For good, this time.' And Guinevere said, 'Fine, leave, Mr Smartypants. I'll help you pack.' And she did."

Ursula smiled, raised her eyebrows. "Good for her. But tell me then, why did Griselda abandon you?"

"She didn't abandon me. She moved to Winnipeg."

"And they don't allow cats in Winnipeg?"

"Of course they allow cats in Winnipeg. But not where she lives."

"Do you hope to see her again, Dufus?"

"I do. Don't ask me when, but I do."

"Is that why you're bound for Lake Street?"

"Yes."

"But you're in no hurry. You say you've been on the road since Thanksgiving. This tells me something. This tells me you don't really believe in your mission. Or else you're having second thoughts. What if she never comes back?"

"She'll come back."

"But what if she doesn't?"

"I haven't thought that far ahead."

"Well, maybe you should. Will you be heartbroken?"

"Disappointed."

"You could always move in here. There's worse places. Mahatma likes you. If only we could get rid of Hermione. It's too bad they demolished that grain elevator. We could have sent her down there."

At that moment, who should arrive on the scene but Hermione herself. She'd been up a tree after goldfinches. She wished us both good morning for the tenth time and called us by name. "I felt my ears burning," she said. "Were you two talking about me?"

Ursula drew herself up, flicked her majestic tail. "Don't flatter yourself, Nosy Parker. We were talking about the woman Dufus used to live with. Her name was Georgina and after evicting her no-account husband she ran off to Winnipeg. Same old story. The grass is always greener. Those left behind pay the piper."

Puzzled, uncomprehending, Hermione frowned, shook her head. "Have you heard the news? The first ship has been sighted in the harbour. It's an early start to navigation. I'll soon be out on my tugboat."

Muttering to herself, Ursula waved her tail grandly. I believe she said, "The sooner the better."

I left Barnabas Safe Haven after breakfast on a sunny, mild March morning. When Ursula saw me ready to go, she said, "Why not stay a little longer, Dufus? Why not stay till Easter? What's your hurry?"

The truth was, I didn't see much point in staying longer. I'd heard all her stories, her flights of fancy, and Hermione's too. For two such similar cats, I wondered why they didn't get along better. "I don't want to wear out my welcome," I said. "Besides, I'm anxious to see Lake Street again. Look up the old gang. Bronco, Grimsby . . ."

"They'll be gone, Dufus. Take my word for it. Cats don't stay put any more. Not like in the old days. Look at you, for example. Walking all the way from Pioneer Drive."

"Skyline Avenue."

"Whatever."

So I went and said goodbye to Mahatma, tried to let him know I appreciated his hospitality. He didn't seem surprised I was leaving. I said goodbye to Hermione, who told me I should stop in at the Hoito Restaurant on Bay Street for a feed of Finnish pancakes. "It's on your way," she said. "You'll find cats galore, especially at this time of year. The Hoito is a meeting place for all the bush cats and farm cats, all the young cats starting out on their own, who come back for old times' sake. You'll find any number of retired ships' cats too. Say hello to them for me. Tell them Hermione sends her love. Tell them if we never meet again this side of Heaven, we shall meet on that beautiful shore. That's from one of the eventide songs they sing here at Barnabas."

It was a short walk to Secord Street, where I turned south. In the parking lot of the Italian Cultural Centre a bearded old man in cap and windbreaker sat on a chair at the entrance, playing an accordion. He had no visible audience, other than dogs and children, but seemed content. From there, I could smell fresh bread being baked at Kivela Bakery, a pleasing, comfortable aroma, though not one that made me drool. I walked along under rattling, leafless birch trees. When I turned the corner on Bay Street I saw a dozen elderly men sitting on benches in front of the Hoito, enjoying the spring sun. They talked and gesticulated, waved their arms for emphasis, seemed intent on whatever it was they were discussing. An ancient De Soto taxicab waited at the curb, its doors open and its driver sprawled across the front seat. People walking by said hello to him, but did not seem interested in hiring his services. They weren't going very far, and were in no hurry to get there.

I might have sat and contemplated this quaint social scene, in which there was no conflict, no controversy, had I not noticed a gathering of small dogs under the trees on the boulevard. As nearly as I could tell, they were under the lax control of a long-haired youth who held their leashes in one hand and spoke sharply to them when they fidgeted. I assumed he was a professional dog-walker, who, instead of walking his dogs, was taking his ease among the assembled Finnish pensioners. He was smoking a cigarette and laughing, but I wondered how nonchalant he'd be if his charges suddenly saw me and gave chase. I imagined the resulting pandemonium, and wondered who the hoary old Finlanders would cheer for.

While I would have liked to stop off at the Hoito, maybe sneak around in back and see if there were any cats cadging handouts at the service entrance, I deemed it more prudent to cross Bay Street and sneak along the back lane toward Algoma. Which I did. Passing the travel agency on the corner, I saw a huge poster in the window showing two silver Ocicats in straw hats and sunglasses, reclining under palm trees on a white sand beach. They had flower leis around their necks and were sipping tall drinks. While the scene looked inviting, especially after such a long, cold winter, I didn't see how regular folk could possibly make the trip. Pipe dreams. Pie in the sky.

Behind the Fireweed Gift Shop I stumbled upon an enclave of cats under a maple tree. I thought I could smell opiates in the air, sweeter than wild mint, as piquant as snapdragons. To this day, I don't know what it was. At first, I thought there was some sort of celebration in progress. But then, around the perimeter, I noticed young people with video cameras. Walking up to a chocolate tabby on the sidelines, I said to her, "What gives?"

"Feline reality show for TV," she whispered. "Film students from Confederation College. 'A Day in the Life of a Bindlestiff.'"

"Of a what?"

"Of a Bindlestiff. Hobo. Drifter. Vagabond. Surely you know the series *Cats on the Prowl.*"

"No, I'm afraid I don't."

"Jeez, you been living under a rock?"

"Yes, in a manner of speaking. My name is Rufus. I'm on my way to Lake Street. What's that smell?"

"Smell? I don't smell anything. If you have a sensitive nose, this is no place for you."

"It smells like narcotics."

"Oh, that. Well, it's entirely possible. I believe Regina, mascot at the Bughouse Bar & Grill across the street, just got in a shipment of Colombian catnip from Juan Escobar, Pablo's son. He's a cat fancier, you know. Always sends high-quality spurge."

"Spurge?"

"Weed. Ganja. Stick."

"I thought Pablo Escobar was dead."

"He is. Dead as a doornail. Since 1993. His son Juan has taken over the cartel. He's the cat fancier."

"I don't know whether to believe you or not. I didn't catch your name, by the way."

"That's because I didn't give it. I make it a rule never to give my name to strangers. In this day and age, you can't be too careful, what with identity theft and all. If you must know, it's Olivia. I'm Regina's cousin. I was bridesmaid at her wedding. I'm also the fiancée of that Himalayan shorthair they're videotaping right now. His name is Rocko. If I were you, I wouldn't let him see you talking to me. He's mean and ornery, with a jealous streak. Be warned, Rube, or whatever the hell your name is."

"It's Rufus. I've just come from Barnabas Safe Haven."

"So?"

"So nothing. I spent a week there. It's an interesting place. I met some interesting cats. Ursula. Hermione."

"It's a nuthouse, Rube. Full of psychos. Did you hear what I just said?"

"About what?"

"About Rocko, my jealous boyfriend."

"Yes, I heard. But I'd like to watch the filming."

"Fine. Watch the filming. Just don't talk to me. Or they'll be filming your funeral. Tell you what. To make it easier, I'll go and sit by the fence. You stay here. If they point a camera at you, smile, but don't say anything. That's their instructions to the actors. Don't say anything. For now, it's a silent movie. They'll add the soundtrack later. By the way, after the shoot, we're all invited to a get-together at the BFI dumpster behind the Bughouse. Why don't you tag along?"

"Thank you," I said. "I may just do that. I haven't let my hair down in ages."

"Jeez, who said anything about letting your hair down? We're civilized here, Rube. Not like the oddballs at Barnabas Safe Haven."

*

TEN
Juan Escobar, the Bughouse Bar & Grill, Britney, Grandma Nelly's Farewell

My memories of that night behind the Bughouse are hazy. Not because of all the Colombian catnip recently received from Juan Escobar in Medellin (although Olivia was right - it was ultra high quality), but because I ate too much, talked too much, met too many weird characters. Most of whom were aspiring actors from the Bay-Algoma Drama Guild. At times that evening, there must have been fifteen or twenty cats in and around the BFI dumpster behind the Bughouse Bar & Grill. I remember being impressed at how Rocko and Regina ripped open green plastic garbage bags, out of which spilled chicken skins, steak bones, baby back ribs. There were lamb chops, exotic meatballs, black olives, soggy crusts of flatbread. We fell on this feast with wild abandon, gorged, slobbered, hissed good-naturedly at each other. There was more food than we could possibly eat, and so we rolled in it, grovelled in it, besmirched ourselves. With potato skins on our heads and feta cheese between our toes, we laughed and poked fun. Overhead, a yellow March moon shone down on us. It was, as I overheard Regina say repeatedly, a full-fledged bacchanal. She urged everyone to try Juan Escobar's newest concoction—powdered day lilies. Gimpy older cats, stuffed to capacity, bellies distended, needed help climbing back over the edge of the dumpster. After dropping to the ground, they could be heard groaning with plenitude as they lay in the Bughouse parking lot or wandered dazedly in circles. These early retirees would be replaced by younger, hungrier cats, who came leaping aboard the dumpster and dove headfirst into the spoils. The only complaint I heard was from a pair of prissy, pouting flits, whom I'd seen being filmed earlier in the day, and who said they were disappointed at the lack of dainty desserts. Other than these two, who couldn't keep their paws off each other, there was no restraint, no sense of decorum. Cats tripped over each other, wrestled, sneezed, stole unguarded tidbits. And yet, because there was so much to eat, there was no real animosity. We all had glazed eyes, cruddy whiskers. I wouldn't have missed it for the world.

Between belches, I had meaningless conversations with cats whose names I quickly forgot. Some asked me who I was, most didn't. I vaguely remember looking into the onyx eyes of a plump Russian Blue named Natasha. She would have been sexy except for the gravy on her chin and the broccoli between her teeth. She told me she deplored all the violence on TV. Wearing a hat of lettuce leaves, reeking of Genoa sausage, she expounded her theory: violence shocks us, then we become inured. In no time, it's not grisly enough. "I'm telling you, Rudolf, if they started throwing babies to pit bulls, we'd look away at first, but then we'd grow jaded, and if we looked away, it would be out of boredom. Know what I'm saying?"

"Oh, absolutely. I know what you're saying. I don't watch much TV, for that very reason."

"Me either. It's too depraved."

"By the way, my name is Rufus."

"Rufus, Schmoofus, what's in a name? Mine's Natalie, but everybody calls me Natasha. Have I seen you here before?"

"I doubt it. I've just arrived. I'm on my way to Lake Street."

"Lake Street? What's the big attraction on Lake Street? Do they have BFI dumpsters?"

"I used to live there. I'm going back to my roots."

Grubbing through a mess of macaroni, Natasha unearthed a fish head. "Going back to one's roots is not always a good idea, Rudy. Places change. People change. Not that you need advice from me, but I'd think twice if I were you."

Just about then, Rocko, Olivia's boyfriend, on top of the heap, burst into song. His voice was strong and not unpleasant, but even so, there were catcalls for him to shut up. Moments later, I noticed Olivia weeping. When I mentioned this to Natasha, she said, "Par for the course, Rudy. Rocko sings when he's blitzed, Olivia cries when she's happy."

We might have talked more, had not a brown Bengali with attitude come between us. She was intent on stealing Natasha's fish head, and Natasha was not about to let her. They growled and snarled at each other, and so rather than watch fur fly, I backed off.

Besides, I'd ingested the remains of so many stuffed peppers that the spices were making my head spin. To say nothing of my stomach. Cats covered in steak sauce were sprawled hither and yon, some on the brink of regurgitation. I judged it was time to leave, before leaving became impossible. Especially when one of the prissy boys, with a sick sense of humour, lisped that he thought he heard the BFI truck approaching. Anyone with half a brain would have known it wasn't true, but even so, it caused consternation.

I remember half-jumping, half-falling out of the dumpster. As I looked for a place to lie down, my nose was assailed by the aromas not of gourmet scrapings, but of powdered day lilies. It was too much. Gastric discomfort replaced euphoria. Glancing up, I saw Natasha peering over the edge. She looked completely zonked, but still had the fish head in her mouth. There was no sign of the brown Bengali. The din from the dumpster was awesome—thumps and bangs and battle cries, like swordsmen at war. Mercifully, in an empty storage shed behind an abandoned tire store on Machar Avenue, despite the lingering smell of rancid rubber, I found temporary refuge. I dragged myself in under a tattered tarpaulin and tried to think calming thoughts. Which wasn't easy. I could still hear the fracas I'd just left, and wondered why no one bothered to call the cops.

I'm ashamed to say I didn't move till the weekend. Thursday, though mild, saw rain, and I was glad to be inside. I slept, stretched, drank water from a puddle near the door. Gradually, my stomach ache subsided. My headache, however, remained. I certainly wasn't hungry. If you'd offered me a bowl of your best stroganoff, I would have declined. Friday afternoon, between showers, I walked as far as the BFI dumpster, just as the BFI truck was hoisting it in mid-air on arms of steel and engorging its contents. Tin cans and empty bottles came rattling down, but fortunately, no cat corpses. Then the truck lowered the dumpster, dropped it on the ground with a hollow clang, and drove away. So much for dining out.

Saturday morning dawned sunny and warm. A sweet southerly breeze was blowing. From my hiding place in the tire store I heard the unmistakable sound of a ship's horn out in the harbour. I thought of Ursula's friend Malcolm, the Scottish Fold at Barnabas Safe Haven, and wondered if the two of them had conspired to win the pool.

Shortly after noon, I set off on the last leg of my journey. As I walked along Cornwall Avenue, feeling the sun on my back and the breeze in my face, I remembered Natasha's words of caution about going home again. This close to Lake Street and the railway tracks, and beyond, the old CNR station and marina, I expected to feel excitement. Strangely, now that I was almost home, I think what I felt was apprehension, or at least uncertainty. This puzzled me. Had I really walked all the way from Skyline Avenue in hopes that Guinevere might be there to welcome me? Well, yes. In fact, that's what had kept me going. Now, facing grim reality, I knew that such hope was ridiculous. I asked myself what I'd do if I arrived at the Bayview Apartments and found no familiar faces. What if, as any number of cats had suggested, I'd made a foolish mistake? What was it Natasha had said? "Places change. People change. If I were you, Rudy, I'd think twice." For the first time in months, I wondered whether I should have stayed on Skyline Avenue.

Well, it was too late now. If there was no one at the Bayview Apartments to take me in, if no one recognized me or knew I belonged to Guinevere, I could at least take comfort in the thought that summer was coming and I'd be able to sleep outdoors. After six months on the road, living by my wits, I knew one thing: I'd become a survivor. Guinevere would be proud of me. That is, if she were there. Which, realistically, I had to admit was unlikely.

Thinking these rather depressing thoughts, I believe I actually slowed my steps. Not consciously, or on purpose, but in spite of myself. I was leery of disappointment. So close to home, when I should have been in a self-congratulatory mood, I was beset by vague fears.

At the corner of Cornwall Avenue and Vigars Street, a neighbourbood dimly familiar to me from my youth, I came upon a peculiar scene. In a shed attached to a ramshackle house, on the back seat of a prehistoric car, whose missing engine and flat tires indicated it hadn't run in years, there were a half-dozen solemn cats grouped around a recumbent, rust-coloured tabby. She looked as old as the car, as old as the tumbledown shed. A sort of bed had been made for her on the car seat, out of which oozed sponge rubber stuffing.

I hadn't meant to stop, but I did. Oddly, the other cats made room for me. They may have thought I was a distant relative. The old cat's eyes were closed. Perhaps sensing my presence, she opened them, looked me over, closed them again. "Peter?" she whispered.

"No," I said. "My name is Rufus. I was just passing by."

I expected the other cats to say something, but they didn't. Finally, the old red tabby, obviously at death's door, whispered, "Why would you change your name, Peter? You're not Rufus, you're Peter, my only son. My first-born. I've been expecting you. Do you know someone named Rufus? Did he send you?"

"My name's not Peter," I said. "My name is Rufus. I'm on my way home to Lake Street. I've been away since October."

Without opening her eyes, the red tabby said, "Such a long way, Peter. Winter's no time for travel. I wanted you to come and see me, and you did. Your doting mother is grateful. Tell me you won't go away again."

I turned to the other cats for help. One of them, a black and white teenager, said, "Nelly is our grandmother. She's dying. Every day, she asks if we've seen Uncle Peter. We haven't. He's her fair-haired boy. To hear her talk, you'd think he was her only child. My mother and my aunt Olga come to visit, but Grandma doesn't recognize them. The only one she wants is Uncle Peter. You look a bit like him."

Nelly's other grandchildren were silent. I don't know why. Perhaps they were mute with grief. Or wished they were elsewhere, or that Nelly would miraculously recover.

"Peter," she whispered, refusing to believe I wasn't him, "do you remember growing up in this garage? You were born on the back seat of this car. In those days, it used to run. Every time they started it up, I carried you and your sisters into the loft. Do you recall the good times we had back then, Peter? Your father, whom I never should have married—never marry a Balinese, everyone said, they'll break your heart—went west in a boxcar before your eyes were open. He promised me he'd be back before the snow flew, but I never saw him again. Now I'm going on a journey too. I told your sisters not to feel sorry when I leave. I intend to enjoy myself. I'll never be cold or hungry again, Peter. I've seen glimpses of Heaven, full of sweet grass and peonies. I've heard birds singing, crickets chirping. Right now, I smell winter roses. No more draughty old sheds for me, Peter. I knew you'd be here when the time came. I knew you wouldn't desert me. You're not your father's son. I wish you'd sing me a song, Peter. Like you used to, when you were a kitten. Remember the one I taught you about the chariot? 'Swing low, sweet chariot, comin' for to carry me home.' Sing it for me, Peter. I know you remember. Or the one about the gospel train. 'Get on board, little children, get on board. There's room for many a-more.' Make your old mother happy, Peter. Before she starts her long journey."

I looked helplessly at the other cats, who, I realized, were all quite young. They offered no help. They had long faces, tear-filled eyes. To them, very quietly, I said, "I'm not Peter. I don't even know this lady. What's more, I don't know any songs about chariots or gospel trains."

"That's all right," the black and white teenager said, stepping forward. "We'll do it."

And they did. They stood close to Nelly, almost touching her, and sang very softly: "I looked over Jordan, and what did I see, comin' for to carry me home? A band of angels, comin' after me, Comin' for to carry me home." And they sang, "The gospel train is comin', comin' round the bend. Get on board, little children, there's room for many a-more."

Whether they actually knew these songs or not, I couldn't say. Though the melodies were pleasing, the youngsters might have been making up the words as they went along. But it was what Nelly wanted. She lay motionless, eyes closed, barely breathing. You could tell she was happy. She'd stopped shivering. Her ears perked up, as though she'd heard a familiar voice. The tip of her tail twitched.

"Now sing about the precious jewels," she whispered.

And they did, very softly: "They shall shine in the morning, His bright crown adorning, They shall shine in their beauty, Bright gems for His crown."

I stayed there all afternoon. Not because I wanted to, or felt needed, but because I couldn't think of a reason not to. Especially when someone said, "When she wakes up, tell her you're Uncle Peter. It would make her happy."

The fact is, I wasn't in that much of a hurry. Unlike Nelly, who had seen a reassuring vision of her future, I was having misgivings. Here, in this decrepit garage, there were fellow cats, albeit strangers, with whom I could converse. At the Bayview Apartments on Lake Street, I might encounter sudden loneliness. Ashamed of my timidity, I stayed because I was afraid to depart. Afraid of what I might find, or not find, on Lake Street. I hadn't yet worked up the courage to complete my odyssey. I did, however, move to the edge of the circle of grandchildren, and discovered a dish of kippers in tomato sauce on the floor. Where it came from,

I couldn't say, but as it was my first meal since the orgy in the dumpster, I partook of it hungrily, alongside the black and white teenager, who chose that moment to inform me that her name was Britney.

When we'd finished eating, she wanted to know why it had taken me so long to walk from Skyline Avenue to Vigars Street. I asked her if she'd ever been to Skyline Avenue, or if she had any concept of the wasteland that lay between. She said she'd never been north of Secord Street, never east of Ambrose. "I'll admit it," she said, "I've led a sheltered existence. But someday, if a knight in shining armour comes along and offers me a ride, I'll take it. I'll venture forth and see the world. It's, like, my fondest hope."

"I wish you luck," I said. "I hope your knight comes by and gets you. But if he doesn't, I wouldn't worry. There's something to be said for staying home and raising a family."

Apparently this was not what Britney wished to hear. "Are you kidding, dude? And be like my mother? Be like Grandma Nelly? Be a dutiful housewife? I don't think so. Stay home and grow old without ever having been anywhere? I really don't think so. It's fine for you men. You take off and leave the little woman at home with six squalling brats. What a rip-off. You sound like my father. Like Uncle Peter. While you're out partying, we're stuck at home, in a rotten old car, in a rotten old garage. We're seeing visions, waiting to die, without ever going anywhere or doing anything worthwhile. No thanks, Romulus, or whatever the hell your name is. For a guy who's just walked halfway across town, you shouldn't be advising people to stay put. I mean, like, give me a break! Practise what you preach, or don't preach."

I was about to counterattack, or at least defend myself, which would have been a waste of time, but was saved from having to do so, because at that moment one of the younger cats said, "I think Granny's gone."

Someone else said, "She's not gone, dipstick, she's right here."

"I mean, I think she's died. Her eyes are open, but they're all white, and she's not breathing."

As before, they stepped aside and urged me forward, as though I were some sort of guru. I started to say, once again, that I didn't know Grandma Nelly, that I wasn't their Uncle Peter. But the sight of that lifeless red cat, lying there curled up, made my protests futile. What struck me was how peaceful Nelly looked, how unafraid. Britney approached her, licked her tired old face, gently closed her eyelids. She said, "You've lived a good life, Granny. Maybe you weren't the prima ballerina, but you were our granny. We shouldn't be sad. You wouldn't want us to be sad. Where you're gone, there's no sadness. We'll miss you, Granny. And we'll be thankful we had such a loving grandmother."

I was ready to leave then, ready to hurry away, and was nearly out the door, when Britney caught up to me. "Come back and see us someday, dude. When your journey's over. You'll be more than welcome, even if you're not Uncle Peter. Come tell us how you're doing. And if you see any knights on white horses, send them my way."

The old buildings on Vigars Street, and the street itself, were bathed in late afternoon sunlight. There was a breeze off the harbour, and when I looked in that direction I saw a thumping red and white icebreaker charging back and forth, belching smoke, cutting channels. Above these blue pathways of open water, the air was full of screaming gulls, harbingers of Easter, harbingers of spring.

As I walked toward Lake Street, familiar landmarks came into view: the casino, the fire station, the stately Chronicle-Journal building. Even the Prospector restaurant on Cumberland Street, where, a long time ago, in happier days, Guinevere and Aristotle used to go for porterhouse steaks and bring home scraps in a doggie bag.

The Bayview Apartments hadn't changed since I'd last seen them. I don't know why, but I expected them to look different. They didn't. The bricks were still slate grey. There were still barbecues and bicycles on the balconies. Fewer flower pots than I remembered, but just as many outdoor clotheslines. I wish I could say I was happy to be home. Happy to see my old neighbourhood. But I wasn't. I was filled with trepidation. Never, during my whole journey, had I felt so alone. I debated turning tail and running back to Vigars Street, where Britney and her gang were in mourning for their grandmother. Yet even there, I would have felt like an outsider. And so I sat on the grass beside Lulu's Hair Salon and tried desperately not to wish I was back on Skyline Avenue with Guinevere's aunt and uncle, or in Theo Godyke's sweet-smelling canoe shed.

Thinking these thoughts, hoping against hope that Guinevere would be in her old apartment, and not in far-off Winnipeg, I watched for a gap in traffic and prepared to cross the street. I remember thinking to myself that if Queenie, who lived up north near the Expressway, could see me now, she'd have to admit I'd grown much better at crossing thoroughfares. In October, she'd called me a bumpkin and said she was surprised not to see me lying in the middle of the road, flat as a pancake. Well, I'd come a long way since then.

*

ELEVEN
Home at Last! Venetia Agrippa and Jailhouse Neville

Guinevere wasn't there. I'd known she wouldn't be. I knew it as I crossed the street, with the setting sun on my right shoulder. I knew it as I looked up at her old apartment on the fourth floor and saw a bicycle on her balcony. Guinevere had never owned a bicycle. Still, I thought maybe she was in there somewhere, in a different apartment. Talk about clutching at straws. Faint hope is better than no hope, I suppose. Better than a panic attack. Oddly, I had no sensation of having completed an odyssey. The only sensation I felt was fear. So far, I'd been lucky. Maybe my luck had run out.

While I sat at the Bayview's entrance, with no immediate plan of action, the widow Agrippa, Guinevere's next-door neighbour, came along with a bag of groceries. She's an intense, talkative lady, with short black hair, a dusky complexion and winning smile. In her prime, I'll bet her dance card was always full. Even now, she still has that certain something. I recognized her immediately, although I don't think she recognized me. Not at first. I'd always liked Mrs Agrippa, but I had the feeling, wrongly, as it turned out, that she was not particularly fond of me. When she used to come to Guinevere's apartment for afternoon tea, she always sat across the room from me. She never patted me, never brought me treats, or said what a handsome cat I was. She mostly talked to Guinevere about her convict son, Neville, imprisoned at Stony Mountain for a variety of crimes, including armed robbery. Or about her late husband, Claudio, who had once held a female teacher hostage for three days in a rural school. The police were afraid to storm the school, for fear Claudio might harm the teacher, as he'd threatened. After three sleepless nights he'd dozed off, the woman had escaped, and the police had flushed Claudio out with tear gas. His reasons for the hostage-taking were never made public, but Mrs Agrippa once told Guinevere he'd demanded a Lincoln Continental and two cases of Old Vienna.

With her bag of groceries in one hand, Mrs Agrippa stepped around me on the sidewalk, adjusted her spectacles, prepared to insert her key in the vestibule door. "You know what?" she said. "You look just like Guinevere's cat. But you can't be. Guinevere doesn't live here any more. She moved to Winnipeg. I had a letter from her at Christmas. So what are you doing here? If memory serves, didn't she send you to live with her aunt and uncle up in Jumbo Gardens? So you can't be her cat. But you look just like him. I forget his name. I'd let you in, but I don't think you belong here. Sorry."

And then, before I could get my act together, she opened the door and went in. Through the glass I watched her go down the hall to the elevators and press the button for her floor. She shifted her bag of groceries to her other hand, gave me a final glance, shook her head.

I sat there, her words ringing in my ears, not knowing what to do. Never had I felt so afraid or dejected. Nor could I face the immediate problem of where to spend the night. I cursed myself for being a fool. I thought of all the nice places I could have stayed, between Skyline Avenue and Lake Street, and I cursed my stupidity. How pleasant would Barnabas Safe Haven have been right then, at that very moment? I'd have no trouble finding my way back to it.

Five minutes later, fighting tears, I looked up and saw Mrs Agrippa coming out of the building again. She no longer had her shopping bag, but still had her coat on. She stopped in front of me, gave me close scrutiny. "The more I look at you, the more you remind me of Guinevere's cat. It's been months since I saw you, but if you're not him, you bear an uncanny resemblance. And if you are him, how did you get here? Are you homeless? You look lost. I'd let you in, but then what would you do? We can't have the place full of stray cats wandering the halls. The superintendent would throw a fit. He's an intolerant man at the best of times. I can't very well take you in myself. I have no cat food, no litter box. Yet you seem a nice cat, and I've been very lonely these past months, since Guinevere moved away. So listen, cat, whatever your name is, I'll leave it up to you. It's your call. I'll open the door, and you can come with me if you want to. If you don't, that's fine. I won't urge you, I won't carry you. If you do come, it's as a temporary guest. If you're out in the cold and need shelter for the night, and just in case you really are Guinevere's cat, though I don't see how you could be, you're welcome to follow me."

Let me tell you, when she opened the door, I didn't follow her. I bolted ahead, before she could change her mind. My tail must have been flying. Never in my life had I felt so grateful to anyone. When the elevator came, I rushed into it, rubbed Mrs Agrippa's ankle with my head, made a fool of myself. "Goodness," she said, touching me for the first time ever, "you're a friendly thing. Maybe you really are Guinevere's cat. But why am I talking to you like you understand me? I'm a silly old lady, talking to a cat. And yet you seem to know what I'm saying. I wonder if you do. When we get upstairs, I'm going to phone information for Guinevere's number and give her a call. I'll ask her where her cat is supposed to be."

I was there when she made the phone call. I would have loved to hear Guinevere's voice. Mrs Agrippa said, "Guinevere, there's a cat in my apartment right now, that I found outside the building when I came home this afternoon, and he looks just like your cat. Which I know is impossible. No, he hasn't a collar. But he seems to know me, and he looks just like your cat. Same fur, same eyes. Yes, he seems to know me. No, he's not what you'd call skinny. He's not fat, but he's not skinny. I think his feet are sore, though. He keeps licking them. Well, but how could it be? I thought you left him up in Jumbo Gardens before you went away last fall. That's miles and miles from here. A cat couldn't walk that far. By the way, what was your cat's name? Rufus? Did you say Rufus?"

When Mrs Agrippa said my name, I jumped down off the chair I'd been sitting on, ran over and rubbed her ankle again. Into the phone, she said, "I think it's him, Guinevere. I think he knows his name. I think it must be Rufus. Why are you crying, child?"

And then Mrs Agrippa did a strange thing. At least, it seemed strange to me. She said to Guinevere, "So you'll call me right back, dear? All right, I'll be waiting. No, I'm not going anywhere. Where would I go?" And then she hung up the phone.

She could tell I was puzzled. Still talking to me as though I understood, she said, "Rufus, Guinevere's going to call her aunt and uncle and get right back to me. She thought you were still on Skyline Avenue. They didn't tell her any different. She thinks maybe they were afraid to. She thinks she knows why they discouraged her from coming for a visit. So she's calling them right now. If you're there, you can't be here, and if you're here, you can't be there. Not unless you're a magic cat. In the meantime, would you like some tuna? I'm afraid that's all I have, unless you prefer lettuce and tomatoes, which I doubt. And if you're staying the night, which it appears you are, I'll give you some torn up newspapers in a box on the balcony, because I'm not going down in the elevator with you after dark. But please don't use my potted geraniums. Not that they couldn't use some fertilizer, but they aren't awake yet."

I was halfway through my tuna, which was very tasty, when the phone rang. I heard Mrs Agrippa say, "Well, I never! Not since Thanksgiving? And they were afraid to tell you? Well, I never! Then it must be him, poor thing. He came right in here like he knew me. No hesitation. Of course he's hungry. He's having supper as we speak. Expensive tuna. No, he's not skin and bones, nor terribly dirty. But like I said, I think his feet are sore. Why on earth wouldn't they tell you he was missing? Well, yes, I'm sure they thought he'd been run over and wanted to spare you. But even so. Well, he's here. No, he's fine. He's had a meal and a drink of water and now he's sitting on my couch, having a bath, looking pleased with himself. He seems to think he belongs here. I'll tell him you said so. And stop crying, dear. Of course you miss him. I'm sure he misses you. But he's fine. No, of course I don't mind. Don't be silly. Two or three weeks? No problem. How many people would fly all the way here from Winnipeg just to see a cat that might not even be theirs? Though I'm sure this one is. If I had a camera, I'd send you a picture, but I don't. I used to, but Neville took it and sold it behind my back. You're lucky, dear. Well, neither did I. But I still say my misfortune with men was worse than yours. One dead, one in jail. That's fine, dear. There's no rush. We'll manage. See you when you get here. Say hello to your new boyfriend for me. The one you mentioned in your Christmas letter. He did? Well, I'm sorry to hear that. Better luck next time. You're still young. There'll be plenty more. You just have to wait for the right one."

I must tell you, it was an interesting three weeks. Naturally, I was anxious to see Guinevere. But I was happy too, knowing she'd come as soon as she had a weekend free, or could take time off. I'll admit I dreamed about her, heard her voice, felt her touch.

One nice thing about Mrs Agrippa was that she was there all day. She didn't have to go out to work, as

Guinevere had done. Another good thing was that she spoiled me. She shopped at Quality Market for cat food and kitty litter. She gave me tasty tidbits off her plate and the occasional dish of ice cream. She let me sleep late, combed my fur, said repeatedly how nice it was to have company in the apartment, someone to talk to while she did the dusting, someone to watch soap operas with. She said that until I came into her life, she hadn't realized how lonely she was, or how much she liked cats. "I should have taken you when Guinevere moved away," she said. "I should have adopted a cat long ago. But I'm glad I waited for you, Rufus. You're so clean and quiet, and you don't get into mischief. Someday I'll tell you about my son Neville, the convict, and his no-account father, who gave me nothing but grief."

Best of all, and the thing I appreciated most, was that as the weather warmed, Mrs Agrippa allowed me to sit out on her balcony. As March gave way to April and ships began steaming into port, she often joined me. We would sit in the sun, watching gulls and pigeons, and while she puttered with her flower boxes, digging up the soil and planting bulbs, I would crouch beside her, pretending to be interested, and give silent thanks. Now and again I scanned the balconies across the courtyard for my friends Bronco and Grimsby, but saw neither hide nor hair of them.

One day, after I'd been with her a couple of weeks, Mrs Agrippa said to me, "Rufus, my boy, you're getting fat and sassy. You're starting to look nice. Nicer than when you arrived, because truthfully, you were a bit ratty back then. But we may soon have a small problem. I'm afraid you may have misunderstood. I'm afraid you may think that Guinevere is coming here to take you back to Winnipeg with her. It's understandable that you should have that impression. But as she told me on the phone the other day, that won't be possible. Or at least, not for quite a while. She still can't have pets where she lives, and she's on a one-year lease. Which won't mean much to you, but for the time being, she can't take you with her. She's not sure she'll ever be able to. Not unless she comes back here to live, and that's not in the cards. So you see what I'm saying? I don't want you to be disappointed. That's why I'm telling you this. I know you don't understand what I'm saying, but you're an intelligent cat, an affectionate cat, a good companion, and I hope you're happy here."

Her voice trailed off, so I've no idea what else she intended to say. We sat side by side in the sun, and as she stroked my fur I purred. Across the courtyard and down a floor, soaking up sun on her own balcony, I noticed another cat, a lovely Seal-point Siamese with sapphire eyes. Like me, she was enjoying the fresh, fishy breeze from Lake Superior. As I watched, she stretched luxuriously, showing off her lustrous coat, her elegant legs and long, unkinked tail. Mrs Agrippa said to me, "I see you've spotted Millicent. Or is that Rebecca? Snooty Mrs Pepperdine has two cats. I never know which is which, unless I see them together. If they're anything like her, they won't give you the time of day. Not unless they want a favour. So don't get your hopes up in that direction either."

Which brings the story of my odyssey to a virtual close. Like Odysseus reaching Ithaca after an arduous voyage from Troy (ten years for him, six months for me), somewhat battle-scarred, but mainly intact, I had reached the Bayview Apartments on Lake Street—my destination when I set out on Thanksgiving weekend. Which goes to show what can be accomplished with a little determination. Whereas Odysseus, according to the tale Guinevere once read to me when I was sick in bed with a fever, arrived home in a fine ship supplied to him by King Alcinous, my dull journey, by comparison, was done entirely on foot. And while red-haired Odysseus, upon his arrival, was reunited with his beloved Penelope, I had not been quite so lucky. Instead of finding Guinevere, I found the widow Agrippa. Still, I couldn't complain. Things had worked out well. And just as heroic Odysseus was given a crown of wild olives and treated to homecoming banquets, so was I. Mrs Agrippa bought me a handsome yellow flea collar, which she said looked good on me, and I spent sunny afternoons on her balcony, lapping salmon juice out of a saucer and ogling the languorous Pepperdine sisters. Talk about the life of Riley.

Speaking of Guinevere, I must give her credit—she sized up the situation quickly. She could see how happy I was to be reinstalled at Bayview Apartments, and how happy Mrs Agrippa was to have me. And so there was no talk of me going to Winnipeg with her, or back to Skyline Avenue, or (perish the thought) to the Hollyland Haven animal shelter.

She arrived on Good Friday and stayed till Easter Monday, during which time we ate mounds of smoked turkey and had a fine, nostalgic reunion. I spent hours in her arms, being carried about Mrs Agrippa's apartment. She'd made a reservation at the Prince Arthur Hotel, just up the street, and would have stayed there, but Mrs Agrippa wouldn't hear of it. She insisted that Guinevere use Neville's old room, sleep in his old bed, and so that's what she did. That's what we both did.

I remember her walking into the apartment that Friday, carrying a small suitcase, and when she saw me she dropped the suitcase, gathered me up, and buried her face in my fur. To Mrs Agrippa she sobbed, "It's him, Venetia! It's really him! I'd recognize the old reprobate anywhere. Oh, Rufus!"

I'd almost forgotten that Mrs Agrippa's name was Venetia, so at first I wondered who Guinevere was talking to. Except for her hair, which was now blonde, she hadn't changed much. A tad thinner, perhaps, and no longer wearing glasses. When Mrs Agrippa mentioned this, Guinevere said she'd had laser treatments in Winnipeg. To please her new boyfriend. Plus a make-over in shoes, hair colour and perfume. None of which, evidently, had been enough to hold him. "Good riddance," said Mrs Agrippa, taking the words right out of my mouth.

We spent most of Saturday and Sunday on the balcony, eating, reminiscing, enjoying the weather. Guinevere held me on her lap and said she wished I could tell them the story of my odyssey—where I'd stayed, what I'd seen. "People must have taken him in, Venetia," she said to Mrs Agrippa. "Fed him, given him shelter. Oh, I wish he could talk. I feel so guilty about leaving him on Skyline Avenue with my aunt and uncle. What if dogs had got him? What if he'd been run over on the Expressway? The worst of it is, we never would have known. Thank you for recognizing him and letting him in. Little wonder he's so happy here with you. You know what I'm wondering? I'm wondering if he understands what we're saying. Wouldn't that be cool? And what if that story of Odysseus I read to him once when he was sick inspired this journey? No, that's silly, isn't it? It couldn't have."

Mrs Agrippa looked doubtful. "He's not the first cat to walk home over a great distance, my dear. Myth or no myth. Still, it's an accomplishment. You have to hand it to him. He's a courageous cat. Foolhardy, but courageous."

Guinevere left us on Monday afternoon to catch her flight back to Winnipeg. A taxi came for her, and we said goodbye on the balcony. It was a sad farewell, but with fewer tears than her arrival. She tried to give Mrs Agrippa money for my upkeep, but Mrs Agrippa wouldn't accept it. I think this was her way of laying claim to me. I was her cat now, not Guinevere's. And if I was her cat, she'd cover my expenses. Guinevere must have realized this, because she didn't press very hard.

She pressed me hard, though. Picked me up and almost crushed me. Told me to behave and not shed hair or barf up fur balls on Venetia's carpet. She said she'd come back in the summer for a visit. She said she would have bought me a fancy collar, but since I didn't need one, thanks to Venetia, she'd see about scoring some Colombian catnip for me instead. She'd heard that Pablo Escobar's son Juan was supplying prairie cats with a brand new treat—powdered day lilies.

And then she was gone.

Just like that. All she left behind was a breath of perfume and the echo of her voice. Mrs Agrippa and I went out on the balcony. While she potted a few geraniums, I chased a pair of pigeons off the railing. Then I lay down for a restorative nap. For some reason, I dreamt not of Guinevere, but of Theo Godyke and his aromatic, cedar-smelling canoe shed. Phyllis, Queenie and Britney were in the dream too, laughing their heads off at something Theo had said about pine-scented coffins and nocturnal admissions.

When I woke up and wandered indoors, Mrs Agrippa was at the kitchen table, composing a letter to her son Neville. "I'm telling him all about you, Rufus, about your amazing odyssey, and Guinevere's visit, and how we spent Easter together. It's not easy being a convict's mother, trying to think up chatty things to say to your son in prison. I'm glad I have your adventure to talk about."

Anything to oblige, I thought. It's the least I can do. No, being a convict's mother, or the wife of a hostage-taker, can't be fun. But then, going on a winter pilgrimage is no fun either. If I had a choice, I'd rather be a canoe-builder. Or the caretaker of a church. I certainly wouldn't want to be a prisoner. Although, come to think of it, most of us are in some sort of prison, aren't we? Even if it's of our own making. There we sit, regretting the past, hoping for letters from our mothers.

And that, as Odysseus supposedly said to Penelope upon reaching the golden shores of Ithaca, and as James Joyce once said, after a walking tour of Dublin, is the story of my journey, as best I remember it.

*

TWELVE
Epilogue

Will wonders never cease? Contrary to what I thought, my story was not quite over. Almost, but not quite.

Yesterday afternoon, as I was sitting out on Mrs Agrippa's balcony, catching a few rays, I heard a familiar voice. Familiar, yet strange. What I mean is, I couldn't quite place it. Not at first. A rich, mellifluous voice. The voice of a large man, who used to talk to me about canoes and coffins. Theo Godyke's voice! I sat up, jumped down off my chair, stuck my head through the railing. No, I said to myself, it's not possible. At last report, Theo and his wife were in Fort Lauderdale. So it can't be him. It only sounds like him. Anyway, what on earth would Theo Godyke be doing at the Bayview Apartments on Lake Street?

And then I saw him. Bearded, abdominous Theo, still wearing his Greek fisherman's cap. He was on the balcony of a nearby fourth-floor apartment, directly across the courtyard. You didn't need telescopic vision. He had some kind of drawing in his hand and was showing it to a man and a woman. Either he or they had just cracked a joke, and all three were laughing uproariously. In my excitement, I almost fell through the railing. I meowed as loudly as I could, making poor Mrs Agrippa come running. Then I meowed again, and yet again, until finally Theo looked across the courtyard and spotted me.

It took a few moments for my identity to register. For him to realize I was not just some tenant's crazy cat meowing for the fun of it. He glanced in my direction, turned back to his drawing, then did a sudden, perfect double-take. I gave him another loud meow, so loud, in fact, that Mrs Agrippa gazed skyward to see if we were under attack. And that's when Theo, shading his eyes, pointed at me and bellowed, "PUSS! PUSS! PUSS!"

I could hear him telling his friends that he thought he knew me. That there couldn't be two cats so similar in voice or appearance. "PUSS!" he shouted. "PUSS, WHAT THE HELL ARE YOU DOING HERE?"

I was wondering the same thing about him.

I saw him ask his friends whose balcony I was on, and the next thing I knew, he'd disappeared inside. Moments later, there was a loud knock at Mrs Agrippa's door, and when she opened it, there stood Theo. Big, burly Theo. Talk about a sight for sore eyes. I ran to him, tail hoisted, and jumped exuberantly into his arms. "Puss, Puss, Puss!" he said, over and over, while Mrs Agrippa stood transfixed, one hand over her mouth.

It must have been a ridiculous scene. I buffed Theo's bearded chin with the top of my head, squirmed in his arms, purred like a gravel crusher. He himself was close to tears. He kept saying, "How the hell did you get here, old buddy? How the hell did you get here? I thought for sure you were dead."

Finally he put me down, and while I rubbed my sides along his ankles, he said to Mrs Agrippa, "I'm sorry to disturb you, ma'am, but as you can see, your cat and I are old pals. Last winter, he lived in my canoe shed on Cornwall Avenue. I don't know where he came from, but when me and the missus left for Florida after Christmas, I turned him over to some nice people, Lester and Magdalena. But when I got home last month they told me he'd disappeared. Just up and vanished into thin air, the first warm day. Damned if I know where he went or how he ended up here. I'm Theo Godyke, by the way. I custom-build cedar-strip canoes. I'm making one for my friend Herbie, your neighbour across the courtyard. He just retired from real estate. It was him sold me my house on Cornwall Avenue. I was showing him sketches when old Puss here hollered at me from your balcony."

Mrs Agrippa sank into a chair, told Theo to call her Venetia. When he sat down on the couch, I jumped into his lap and could smell sweet cedar on his clothes.

"Rufus is not really, truthfully, my cat," Mrs Agrippa said. "Well, I suppose he is now. He used to belong to my friend Guinevere, who left him with her aunt and uncle on Skyline Avenue when she moved to Winnipeg last summer. They lost track of him at Thanksgiving. Never saw him again. So that's where he came from. He was on his way back here. He must have walked to your place. I'm not surprised he didn't stay with your friends Lester and Magdalena. He knew he still had a long way to go. When he showed up here three weeks before Easter, I couldn't believe it. I let him in, phoned Guinevere, and she couldn't believe it either. She flew here on Good Friday to make sure it was really Rufus. Which it was. Now he lives with me, and seems happy with the arrangement. So now you know where he came from and where he was going. He's a determined little cat, is old Rufus. By his reaction to you, I'd say you must have treated him well. I believe he's thanking you."

Theo scratched me behind the ears, stroked my fur. "I didn't know his name was Rufus. I just called him Puss. But Rufus suits him. He reminds me of a cat I used to own, Custer. That's why I took him in when he showed up at my canoe shed one miserable rainy day. I thought maybe he was Custer reincarnated."

Mrs Agrippa stood up, shook her head in wonderment. "Would you care for a glass of sherry, Mr Godyke? I have a bottle of Harvey's Bristol Cream I've been saving for a special occasion, and what could be more special than this?"

"I'd love a glass of sherry," Theo said. "And you must call me Theo. It's what my friends call me. Are you a married lady, Mrs Agrippa?"

"If I'm to call you Theo, then you must call me Venetia. I'm a widow, Theo. I've been a widow these many years. You're lucky to have a wife to accompany you to Florida."

Which made Theo smile an odd, rueful smile. Almost a grimace. "I'm not as lucky as you might think. In fact, I'm not lucky at all. In the realm of matrimony, I'd say I'm the unluckiest man alive. If it wasn't for my canoes, I'd be off my rocker."

Curled up on his lap, I wondered if he planned to tell her about his night-time trysts in the yellow pine coffin, or that he chewed unlit cigars. But of course he didn't. He did hold out his glass for a refill, though, and settled himself more comfortably on the couch. "This here wine is very tasty, Venetia. I'd forgotten how much I like Harvey's Bristol Cream. It's dry, but not too dry, sweet, but not too sweet. It's perfect. You can even taste the brandy casks they store it in, over there in Spain. Or is it Portugal? One of them foreign countries. Nothing but the finest oak."

"Just imagine, Theo. Rufus walked all the way from Skyline Avenue. And how good to know he found shelter for Christmas. I'm going to write my friend Guinevere a letter and tell her all about you. And about your canoes. She'll be tickled pink. I'll write to my son Neville as well. I hate to tell you, but he's doing time at Stony Mountain. He needs all the cheering up he can get. Rufus sleeps in his old room, on his old bed. Sometimes I call him Neville by mistake. A convict's life is not easy, and being a convict's mother is not easy either. In fact, it's a heavy burden, I assure you. But you'd hardly know anything about that, would you, Theo? Another sherry?"

Theo eagerly extended his empty glass. "Don't mind if I do. So listen, Venetia, could I, with your kind permission, drop in from time to time and pay my old friend Rufus a visit?"

Mrs Agrippa topped up their glasses. "What a splendid idea. Rufus and I would be delighted. We'd consider it an honour. If you have time and your wife doesn't mind, why don't you come for lunch? I'll make sandwiches. Now that the weather's nice, Rufus and I love to picnic on the balcony. He pretends he could catch a bird if he wanted to."

Which made Theo nod his head and smile. Not ruefully, this time, but as though the idea of me catching a bird amused him.

The bottle of Harvey's Bristol Cream was almost empty before he remembered he was supposed to be showing canoe sketches to Herbie across the courtyard. He stood up, placed me on the couch, and said he'd be back very soon, and often, now that he knew where I lived. After thanking Mrs Agrippa for the wine and conversation, and for filling him in on the parts of my trek he was unfamiliar with, he departed.

And that is truly the end of my story. Except to say that no sooner had Theo left than Mrs Agrippa phoned Lulu's Hair Salon for an appointment and added Harvey's Bristol Cream to her shopping list. Oh, and rooted through her closet for her best summer frocks. Then she and I went out on the balcony, with nothing more pressing to do than enjoy the afternoon.

*

MEMBER OF SCABRINI GROUP

Québec, Canada
2006